MW01229438

THE SCARY ME

THE SCARY ME

Andre R. Whittle

LENNORD COUNTY LIBRARY

"HORROR SECTION"

(SHELF VII)

THE SCARY ME—SHELF VII

ISBN: 9798396978492

INTRODUCTION

Welcome to the Lennord County Library.
This library consists of four sections:

[MUSIC] [PAINTINGS] [VHS] [BOOKS]

Let us visit the book section.

This section is divided into 10 other sections, these sections are:

[HEARTFELT] [THRILLER] [COMEDY] [MYSTERY]

[ROMANCE] [DRAMA] [HISTORY] [FANTASY] [ADVENTURE]

[HORROR]

Let us now visit the

"HORROR SECTION"

This section has nine shelves, and each shelf has nine books. In total,
there are 81 stories.

of

suspense, betrayal, greed, bullying, cunning, freak accidents, gore, sex,
murder, politics, scamming, neglect, confusion, insanity, curiosity, church
culture, voodoo, science, narcissism, drug usage, unusual tendencies,
harsh reality.

And this is Shelf VII.

TABLE OF CONTENTS

SHELF VII

[THE RAMEN CUP NOODLE]

Have you ever met anyone who took hygiene to a whole other level? If not, then let me tell you about a man named Richard P. Benson.

This man is so clean he doesn't even leave his house if it means dirtying his shoes. Richard keeps two socks at his front door, which he puts on whenever he gets home. He likes to take his shoes off in the house; he takes both socks and shoes off at the same time, then washes his shoes in the bathroom sink, and then washes the bathroom sink with bleach. This man spreads his bed the moment he wakes up, he sweeps 24/7, and he even cleans up after his mom, who Richard is living with. His mom is the type who is always leaving beer bottles and cigarette butts all over the house. Richard's mom has never had a problem with him when it comes to tidiness; the only problem she has with her son is his silent ways, the having no friends, the lack of social activities, the countless times you could hear her telling him to "go out more," often, but unfortunately, Richard would rather stay home and clean.

Richard P. Benson, 43 years old, standing around 5 feet 9 inches tall, pale white skin, with freckles, receding hairline, his hairline almost at the middle of his head—but for some reason, the hair at the side of his head did not recede but grew, and he walked with a hunch due to the accident at his former employment—a company called "GenPac."

Richard is receiving disability income from the government: every month, Richard gets $700 on a check in the mail due to a certain incident that happened seven years ago at GenPac Foaming Company. It was April 1982.

GenPak, the number one foaming company in Midtown Lennord County, had three main buildings that were adjacent to each other, had over two thousand workers, consisting of five managers and ten supervisors, and the rest were just laborers. This company made Styrofoam cups and plates; Richard was responsible for the cutting up and burning of unused Styrofoam that was no longer good for production—often, you could see him switching different box cutters due to the amount of cutting he did.

One day Richard was cutting and burning as usual when another coworker yelled,

"Yo! Richie, watch out, to Bomboclaat," said a very tall black man with dreadlocked hair.

He was operating a forklift, carrying rolls of thick foam material. He drove by Richard, the forklift leaking engine oil. The operator had no idea; he pressed on while he flashed his dreadlocks.

"Alright, Richie mon, miwi see you lata," he said.

"Later, Phillip," said Richard in a very lethargic voice.

Richard, still standing there in front of the blazing fire, continues to cut, throw, and burn; the oil is now slowing down, running towards Richard's feet. Richard still hadn't noticed the oil on the floor, the fire still blazing. Richard then turned around, stepped in the oil, and had a very bad fall. Richard fell on his back really hard, hurting his back really bad. His injury was so severe he was put out on disability, and ever since then, Richard hasn't returned back to work. Now back to the year 1989.

Richard P. Benson, now living from his disability money, doesn't even buy much—his mom is the one who spends most of the money; she is the one who has to buy his clothes, too. Richard is always seen dressed in baggy polo shirts tucked in his baggy slacks, his belt always drawn tight at his waist, leaving the front part of his pants in a buckle with the button of his pants always under the belt because he pulls it too tight. He often wears long light brown trench coats when he must go anywhere; he wears glasses when he reads; when Richard is seen in glasses, this is how he looks:

He had a big forehead because of his receding hairline to match his big reading glasses, hair at the side of his head, and white freckled skin. But despite all of that, Richard is very well-mannered, never disrespecting his mom or anyone else. He just doesn't talk a lot, and most people think that is weird—well, except for his mom.

Cassandra Benson, white trash, as they put it: her husband had left her, never to return; he has been gone since Richard was 5. Cassandra is about 5 feet 2 inches tall, with short black/red hair, red cheeks, and a cigarette always in her mouth. Cassandra is always seen wearing large white baggy shirts with no pants whenever she is home, is mostly drunk, and stays out a lot. At the pub is where you can find her, given that she is a waitress for Midtown local pub. It was

TUESDAY, NOVEMBER 8, 1989

Cassandra is getting ready to leave for work; it is 3 p.m. in the afternoon. There she stands in her room—where she takes her big shirt off, you can see her big belly as it rolls. She then grabs her black plants and black button-up, which is what the Midtown Pub requires her to wear. She then grabs her cigarette and car keys, rushing out the door.

"Hey, Richie honey, I will be going grocery shopping later, so if you want anything now, just order it on my card, okay?" says Cassandra.

"Okay, Mom," says Richard as he gets comfortable on the couch, which has several different color cloths, looking like knitted tapestries, hanging over the top: a red, a blue, and a burnt orange.

Fun fact about Richard: whenever Richard is not cleaning, he spends most of his time watching heartfelt movies, movies that make him cry— this is something he never shares with anyone. You could say he has a warm spot for warmth.

Home alone sitting on his couch, watching the movie called "Adam,"—you know, that movie about the 6-year-old boy that disappeared one day while shopping with his mother at Sears.

There he sits, VHS facing him, TV with the big back, color going in and out.

The movie is now at the scene of the disappearance of young Adam Walsh. Richard starts to feel deep sympathy for the boy's mother. Moments after watching the movie, Richard gets hungry, goes to the kitchen, and searches the cabinet; there is nothing in the cabinet but one Ramen Cup of Noodles. It is chicken flavor. Richard grabs the cup noodle, lights the kettle, and moments later, the kettle comes to a boil. He pours the water into the cup of noodles and then goes back to watch the movie. He puts the cup of noodles on the TV standing, giving it 3 minutes to cool, and presses play. Three minutes later, he grabs the cup of noodles, rips that greasy paper cover, sticks in the plastic fork, stirs, and starts eating the noodles. The movie is now coming up to a very sad part, the part where Adam Walsh was found dead, in a drainage canal alongside Highway 60, Yeehaw Junction, in rural Indian River County, Florida. Richard starts to cry and gets extremely upset— so upset that he tosses the cup of noodles across the living room into the kitchen, hitting the wall and then straight into the garbage can, some of the noodles going behind the garbage can, like, a big chunk of it.

Moments later, after the movie ends, Richard calms down and is now coming back to his senses. He looks down at the floor; he sees the noodle water on the floor: some even got on the Persian rug that lies under the couch; the soup water leads all the way to the kitchen and straight to the garbage can. Richard's cleaning senses activate immediately, and the 43-year-old starts to panic like a 5-year-old: he screams, quickly grabs the mop, and starts to wipe. Wiping the floor aggressively, he cleans from where the soup water had started, wipes all the way to the garbage can, and then Richard realizes the cup noodle is already in the garbage can.

"Nice shot," he says to himself.

He continues to clean. A couple of minutes later:

"Oh! No! I'm Late!" says Richard as he looks at the clock on the wall.

"I can't be late," he says.

You see, Richard is running late for his book meeting at the Lennord County Local Library, called the "Midtown Library."

That's right, Richard is part of a local book club, the one and only activity he does outside the house. Richard does indeed enjoy every meeting; he meets every Tuesday and Thursday night at the library; this book club consists of five other people—two males and three females—and Richard makes six.

Moments later, it's now 4:45, and the meeting starts at 5 p.m., and it takes a 10-minute drive to get to the library from where Richard lives. Richard is now making his way to the book club; already there are Jenny, Alice, Sarah, Kevin, and Murphy; they form a circle, sitting in low metal chairs. Richard steps in, and they all greet him.

"Hey, Richie," says Alice.

A 44-year-old white woman, who works at the Library with Jenny and Murphy, Alice is wearing a black blouse with white stripes tucked into her green skirt, which covers her knee. She has thick calves and vivid shin bones that run down to her black heels; she wears big glasses with messy black hair that sometimes falls over her glasses. She has a boney face with high cheekbones—and a secret crush on Richard. Richard sits down.

"So, what are we reading today?" asks Jenny, who is also white, and 44, like Alice. A slim-bodied white woman, she is wearing a white blouse with the top buttons loose, showing her cleavage. She has a long black scarf tied into a bow around her neck that stretches down to her waist. Her blouse is tucked into her light brown corduroy skirt that covers her knee; she wears black heels as well and is the leader and founder of the book club.

"I don't know, but isn't it Weirdo's turn to pick a book to read?" says Kevin.

Kevin Kowalski, the youngest member of the book club, Kevin is 21, white, and the nephew of Jenny, who forced him to join the book club. Kevin stands 6 feet tall with tall black hair, which he puts in a ponytail. Kevin is wearing light blue jeans, a white sleeveless undershirt, with a black Lennord County High School jacket with a green LC symbol. Kevin had kept his jacket even though he had graduated years ago. He also openly dislikes Richard for being what he calls weird.

"So, what are we reading today, Richie?" asks Alice as she smiles at Richard. Richard smiles back with a blush.

"Well, I have this book called 'Spilled Milk,'," says Richard.

"Isn't that the book about the molested little girl?" asks Kevin.

"Yes," says Richard.

"Well, we don't want to hear none of that," says Kevin.

"Let him read what he wants to read, Kevin," says Jenny. "But, Aunty," says Kevin.

"What did I say?" says Jenny.

"Fine," says Kevin as he looks at Murphy, the only black person in the club.

"Take it easy, Kevin," said Murphy. Age 32, skin faded haircut, currently wearing a white turtleneck with a deep v-cut black vest, with blue jeans, occasionally hangs out with Kevin, and secretly fucking Jenny.

Richard now starts to read the novel, and while he's reading, Kevin grabs his Evian water bottle that is standing right beside the right front leg of his chair. He quickly opens the bottle, and Kevin starts to gulp the water down, making this horrible swallowing sound as Richard reads. Everyone is now looking at Kevin; Jenny turns her head away.

"Kevin, could you not do that?" says Sarah Baker.

A skinny white woman around 31 years old with long black hair, black lipstick, a skinny face, high cheekbones, and expensive perfume, she is wearing a tall, frail black dress that sometimes gets stuck in her butt cheeks so that you can see her round butt pointing out when she walks or when she stands up. She is wearing a black leather jacket, zipped all the way up to her neck, looking like a turtleneck, with her white Converse sneakers. She secretly doesn't want to be there but has to because her parents are writers, and she is trying to impress them. Also, she knows Kevin secretly wants to fuck her; 'Could be why he behaves like that,' she often thinks.

Kevin ignores Sarah.

"I wasn't talking to you," Kevin says to Sarah as he continues to gulp the water.

He finishes the water and crumbles the bottle, making a crushing sound, interrupting Richard's reading. Richard ignores Kevin and continues to read.

Kevin then throws the bottle on the floor. Then the strangest thing happens.

Richard instantly stops reading and starts freaking out—a major freak out.

"Please pick it up! Please pick it up!" he says to Kevin while he stares at the water bottle shaking his hand. "Please pick it up, Kevin," he says while slowly raising his head. Richard is now intensely looking at Kevin, his face turning red—you can hardly see his freckles.

"Or what?" Kevin asks as he looks at Richard, pants all bundled up due to the tightness of his belt. Kevin shakes his head.

"Nothing, just please pick it up, please, Kevin," says Richard in a kidlike voice.

Jenny then picks the bottle up. "Okay, continue, Richard," she says.

Richard then sits back down, picks the book up, and looks at Kevin.

"Pig," Richard says to Kevin.

"Who the fuck are you calling a pig?" says Kevin.

"Ignore him, Richie," says Alice.

"Oh, so you think you are Mr. Clean?" Kevin asks.

"I'M CLEAN!" says Richard VERY LOUDLY!

Kevin doesn't like that Richard is talking to him that loudly in front of everyone; he gets up, hawks the phlegm from the back of his throat, and spits right in front of Richard. Richard starts freaking out again—it gets worse. He quickly drops the book and runs straight out the library door. Richard has gone home.

"What the hell was that, Kevin?" Jenny asks.

"Aunty, he is weird and acts like he is better than us, and he is ugly as hell," says Kevin. She then got up.

"You need to apologize to Richard," says Jenny. "Alice and Murphy, let's go back to work; this meeting is over."

"About time," says Sarah, as she looks at Kevin with disgust and walks off, as Kevin looks at Sarah's ass in her black dress stuck between her ass cheeks.

"I like that ass so much," he says to himself.

Moments later, Richard is getting home; surprisingly, his mom is already home, drinking, smoking a Dosal cigarette, and as usual, making a mess in the kitchen, leaving a plate full of peanut butter and jelly with the knife on top of the plate, which is also messy with jelly. Richard quickly drops everything and goes straight to washing the dishes. His mom sees this and looks at him.

"Richard, honey, I know you like to see the place spotless all the time, but you have to calm down sometimes honey," says Cassandra.

He looks at her as he washes, "I know, Mom, but I'm fine," he says.

"I'm serious, honey; being too much of a clean freak could be the death of you; you will overthink everything," she says.

"Okay, Mom," says Richard.

"Okay," she says as she continues to speak.

"I will be heading back out shortly to do some grocery shopping—do you need anything special?" she asks.

"No, Mom," he says as he continues to wash.

"Are you okay, Richard? Did something happen at your meeting today?" she asks.

"No, Mom, I'm okay," Richard replies.

"Okay, Richard, I will see you in a few hours then," she says.

"Okay, Mom," he replies.

Moments later, Cassandra is now making her way to Price Chopper on 511 Schutt Road.

Richard is now relaxing, watching "Rain Man." The 43-year-old is now sitting in total silence, nothing but the movie playing. Then Alice flashed in his mind; he smiled and continued to watch the movie. "Oh, Alice," he said.

Now let's visit Alice and the others.

Jenny, Alice, and Murphy have decided to pay Richard a surprise visit due to what Kevin has done. They all feel deeply sorry for Richard. They pull up to Richard's house, park on the street, and quickly get to the door. By now, Richard is still watching "Rain Man," the TV playing loudly.

"Serious injury book is a red book; that book is blue," says someone from the movie.

Richard nods his head at what the guy in the movie says; then, he hears a knock on the door. Richard is startled because he knows that his mom doesn't knock, and it's too late for the mailman. He gets up, walks to the door, looks through the peephole, sees Alice's face, and smiles; he quickly opens the door. He is surprised to see Jenny, Murphy, and Kevin sitting in the car parked on the street. Richard looks at Kevin; Kevin looks away with a frown.

"What are you guys doing here?" Richard asks everyone.

"We are sorry for what Kevin did, so we all came to apologize," says Jenny as she stares at the two socks at the door.

"It's fine; I just want to be alone right now," says Richard.

"Can we come in, please?" says Alice as she stares at Richard.

"Kevin, get over here now!" Jenny shouts.

Frustrated, Kevin is now making his way out of the car while the others make their way into the house.

They all get in and look around his house. Alice stares at Richard's heartfelt VHS and book collection. She grabs one of the books from Richard's shelf of books.

"*How To Raise Child* by Andre Paul," says Alice to herself as she looks at the book. The book cover is a picture of a little black boy in a turtleneck and a black man standing next to him, who can also be seen wearing a black turtleneck with a ruler made of blood, sweat, and tears. "Who is this author?" she asks.

"Oh, he is nobody; can you put that back, please?" Richard says to Alice.

"Andre Paul—you don't know who that is?" Jenny asks Alice.

"I don't know who that is," says Alice as she puts the book back in its place.

"He is that local writer from Sage Town who doesn't publish his books—he only writes them for his wife," says Jenny.

"Isn't he the one they say is related to Lennord Junior," says Murphy.

"You mean our beloved founder is related to this Andre Paul guy?" asks Alice.

"Yes," says Jenny.

"Then how did you get that book, Richard?" Murphy asks. They all look at each other.

Kevin then steps in; everyone turns around to look at him. "Finally," says Jenny.

"What?" says Kevin as he looks around Richard's home. "Richard, you are really a clean man," he says.

"He is really clean," says Jenny as she looks at Kevin with disgust.

They line up in the living room. "What are you watching," Alice asks. "Rain Man," says Richard.

"Oh man, Richie, you really love these heartfelt stories," says Jenny. Then suddenly, Kevin gets a phone call on his phone. He answers and steps away from the conversation.

Kevin is now in the kitchen; as he talks on his phone, he suddenly looks down at the floor and sees the noodles behind the garbage can.

"Hey, let me call you back," he says to the person on the phone. He quickly gets off the phone, pulls the garbage can away, and sees the nasty noodles on the floor sticking to the wall, which look like they've been there for hours. He smiles.

"You nasty fuck!" he shouts. Everyone turns around to look at Kevin.

"Who are you talking to?" asks Jenny.

"Everyone, come look at this," says Kevin. They all walk over in a rush, see the noodles on the ground, and get disgusted. They all look at Richard.

"What?" Richard asks as he stands in front of the TV, looking at them in the kitchen, staring down at the floor.

"You act like you are the cleanest person on earth, and you have noodles behind your garbage can. Decaying!" says Kevin. "And you want to call me a pig," he further says.

"What are you talking about?" Richard asks. As he looks at them, he walks over and sees the noodles on the floor.

"I can explain," he says.

"We don't want to hear anything, nasty weirdo," says Kevin. "Get the fuck out of here, nasty man," he says further. Kevin carries on and on, jeering and mocking Richard.

"Kevin, please stop; you were here to apologize to Richard, remember," says Jenny.

"Aunty, fuck this guy. Why do you even have him in the club?" says Kevin. Everyone is looking at Richard as Kevin mocks him.

"Fuck off, nasty man," he says.

"I'M LEAVING THIS NASTY FUCKING PLACE," says Kevin.

Richard is now freaking out. "Get out of my house," says Richard. He says it very sternly. But Kevin continues to mock him while he walks away.

"Nasty! Nasty! Nasty! Ass! Weirdo," he says. All the others follow him and walk out as well, with all their backs turned.

Richard looks at the kitchen counter and sees two old box cutters he had taken from his job seven years ago. He grabs one of them and slides the blade up with his thumb. You can hear the gritty sound it makes as he pushes the blade up—the blade still sharp as ever. Richard quickly walks up and slices Kevin on the back of the neck. Kevin frightens, holds the back of his neck, then turns around.

"What the fuck was that?" he asks.

"Oh my God, Kevin, you are bleeding," says Jenny.

"Why would you do that?" says Murphy as he holds Kevin's neck. Kevin's phone falls out of his pocket.

"We have to get him to a hospital," says Jenny.

"Oh, you're going to jail, asshole," says Murphy as he holds the back of Kevin's head.

Richard is standing still, with the box cutter in his hand, not moving, just looking at Kevin, bleeding out from the neck.

Moments later, Jenny and the others take Kevin to the emergency room. After getting to the hospital, it turns out that it isn't a serious injury. Kevin ends up getting a few stitches, and that was it. He also decides not to press charges against Richard.

Now Jenny, Alice, and Murphy are at the hospital with Kevin, standing beside his hospital bed.

"Can you bring me my phone? It's in my Lennord County jacket," says Kevin to Murphy.

"You kind of deserve this; you know that, right?" Jenny asks Kevin.

"Yes, I know. He probably thinks I will call the cops," says Kevin.

"So, call him and tell him not to worry," says Alice.

"Yes! Murphy, where is the phone?" he asks Murphy.

"That is very grown up of you, Kevin," says Jenny.

"Well, I almost lost my life," he says.

"Your phone isn't here," says Murphy.

"Damn, it must have fallen out at his house. Aunty Jenny can you go get it for me?" says Kevin.

"Okay. Alice, please come with me," she says.

Moments later, Jenny and Alice are now making their way back to Richard's house, driving slowly; it takes about 20 minutes to get there from the hospital.

Cassandra, now getting home from Price Chopper with the car full of groceries, parks out front and steps into the house; the blood was already cleaned up, with no trace of it.

"Richie, honey, can you go get the groceries in the car, please?" she says.

"Okay, Mom," says Richard. As he now gets up.

"Okay, and I'm a little tired, so I will be on the couch if you need me," she says.

Cassandra, now walking past the garbage can, sees the ramen noodles still on the floor. It looks like Richard has missed it again.

"Honey, clean those noodles up; it looks nasty," she says.

Then suddenly, Richard makes a complete stop and pauses in front of the front door. He starts shaking and shivering. He bites his lips, closes his eyes, then walks off. Cassandra is now chilling on the couch as she lies down peacefully.

One by one, Richard takes the groceries into the house and doesn't even wear the two socks he had at the door; on his way out for the second to last bag, Cassandra speaks to him again about the noodles.

"Honey, clean that up before you take anything else in; I said it was fucking nasty. Clean it up now," she says, drunk as hell. Richard then stops at the doorway with the door wide open.

Jenny and Alice arrive, and they park on the street. They see Richard standing at the door and the trunk of the car open in the driveway. They drive down the block to turn around.

Richard then walks off to fetch the rest of the groceries—it's the last two bags. He slams the trunk down shut and goes back inside.

Jenny and Alice are now making their way back up. They park on the road, come out, and start walking toward Richard's house. They walk up to the window, and that is when they witness what happens next.

Richard walks over to his mom, holds her head tightly on the armrest of the couch, then takes his box cutter out from his pocket. Cassandra, with no way to escape, starts to fight. Jenny holds her mouth as she watches,

Richard slowly pushes the box cutter blade up—the blade still sharp as ever—and that is the moment that Jenny and Alice see Richard slice his mom's throat. He slices her throat rapidly; as she screams out, he cuts deeper and deeper. Cassandra is bleeding all over the couch; she is now shaking and shivering.

Then Richard stands up, looks over his mom, and says, "Why don't you clean it up, you fat fucking bitch?" he says, while he slices her throat some more.

"You go fucking clean it up," he says. Cassandra's body is now sputtering for life; Richard goes and grabs the dirty noodles and pushes them straight down her throat. That is when Alice screams out. Richard was startled.

When he looks through the window, his eyes make four with Alice's. They all now stare at each other, and Jenny and Alice take off running,

Then a sudden vibration comes on Kevin's phone; it's a message.

Richard pays it no mind, puts the phone back in his pocket, quickly runs out, and gets in his mother's car. By now, Jenny and Alice are both driving at full speed; Richard starts to drive them down. Then another text comes in on Kevin's phone.

It's from Sarah Baker. Richard pulls over. As he watches Jenny and Alices drive away, he opens the message. It reads, "Hey Kevin, I like the way you have everyone fooled, no one knows we fucking, you turn me on when you give it to that weirdo Richard, you make me so horny when you behave vulgarly, please come fuck me tonight."

Richard sees this and gets extremely mad, and he screams out, then he sends back a message to Sarah. The message says:

"HEY SARAH, DO YOU MIND SENDING ME BACK YOUR ADDRESS AGAIN? LOVE KEVIN,"

[THE COINCIDENTAL JOKE]

Sometimes it's better not to tell a certain joke, a joke that you are uncertain of. There are a lot of sensitive people out there; plus, it's impossible to know who is sensitive or not, and trust me, sensitive people can be dangerous people. This story is about a young, trying comedian who told a good joke—or better yet, he told a really bad joke.

Andy Fraser, age 26, born in Illinois, moved to Lennord County at age seven and has been living in King Town ever since. Standing at 5 feet 10 inches tall, with a mid-cut afro hairstyle that he often patted down in a nice circular shape, thick black eyebrows, a thick black mustache, a clean-shaven face, and fairly dark skin. Andy was a struggling comedian who lived with his wife and son and worked full-time at the Lennord County plant, making $8.00 an hour. He started this job shortly after getting his GED at BOCES. You see, Andy didn't finish high school due to his girlfriend's pregnancy at the time.

When Andy wasn't working at the plant, he tried comedy at night at a local pub in King Town called "Shooter's Pub." Shooter's Pub was the only place Andy performed, but over time it seems Andy had grown tired of the place and often thought of spreading his wings since he believed his talent needed to be seen by others.

Andy Fraser—the man with the brightest smile you've ever seen—was very sharp with his comebacks. He knew how to reach a broad audience with trenchant observations and storytelling. But there was something else that was bothering the young comedian: Andy was struggling to find out-of-the-box jokes; he thought everyone was doing the same jokes every night, and it was now played out. It was

NOVEMBER 1990

Andy was home thinking and pandering about creative jokes, and after not getting anywhere, he decided to take his son for a walk at the park, which was just a couple blocks away from his house.

"Franklin, let's take a walk to the park, buddy," said Andy. This was about 11 in the morning—his wife Cedella was mandated and had to take an extra shift and would not be getting off until 12 pm.

"Okay, Dad," said Franklin, who was watching Saturday morning cartoons— "Paw Paw Bears."

Franklin Fraser was nine years old, with low cut trim, neatly edged, black eyebrows, round puffy cheeks, blue jeans, and a big red and white Reebok sweater with Converse shoes.

Moments later, Andy and Franklin made their way to the park, strolling down the street of King Town.

After starting to walk, Franklin realized that his dad was talking to himself and looking out into space. Franklin squeezed his dad's palm.

"Dad, are you okay?" Franklin asked, looking up at his dad.

"Yes, son, why did you ask?" Andy asked Franklin.

"Well, Mrs. Lawrence said people who talk to themselves are crazy people," said Franklin.

Andy looked at his son and laughed. "Is Mrs. Lawrence your teacher?" he asked.

"Yes, so are you a crazy person, Dad?" Franklin asked.

"No, son, I'm just thinking out loud," Andy said as he laughed some more.

"You mean, you are talking in your mind, but it comes out in words without you knowing?" Franklin asked.

"Yes, Franklin, that is right," said Andy.

"So, because I'm nine, you think you can't talk to me about stuff like this, so you'd rather talk to yourself?" he asked his dad.

"Well, kind of. You see, son, what I'm thinking about, no child would ever understand," he said.

"How do you know that, Dad?" he said.

Andy looked at his son in awe.

"You know, you get everything from your mom, always having surprising insights, but you are too young to understand what I'm saying, though, Franklin," said Andy.

Then Franklin saw the swing in the park. "The Swing!" he said in a hurry as he walked past the jungle gym at the entrance. "Dad, come push me, please," he said.

"Sure, son," Andy replied, patting down his afro.

Forward, backward, forward, backward, forward—that is the motion the swing swung, Andy pushing Franklin at a fast speed, Franklin laughing in total enjoyment. No one in the park but them when suddenly an old Mexican couple with a little girl, around four years old walked over to the jungle gym.

Andy slightly looked at them; the old lady was a little overweight, standing about 5 feet tall with tall curly hair and light skin, wearing a full black outfit; the old man was bald-headed, light skin, dressed in black as well, with a big belly, standing around 5 feet 7 inches.

Andy stood upright as he pushed Franklin—with every push, he thought of Franklin's smartness earlier. Suddenly, he stopped. Franklin looked at his dad.

"Why did you stop, Dad?" Franklin asked.

"Let me ask you something, Franklin," he said as he held on to the chains of the swing.

"Sure, Dad," said Franklin.

"You know, I do comedy every Saturday night, correct?" he asked Franklin.

"Dad, I watch you leave the house every night in your suit; yes, I know that, dad," said Franklin. "You are silly, Dad," he said further. Andy laughed.

"Okay, so my jokes are always about storytelling, which is good, but everyone else is doing that now, so I need something new. What should I do?" he asked Franklin.

"I don't know, Dad, but at school, whenever I tell jokes about myself, the kids laugh more.

"Like what?" Andy asked.

"Well, one day at school, Mrs. Lawrence made us all introduce ourselves. She said we all needed to say something about ourselves. She picked me first, and I got nervous, so I did the one thing I know how to do, the one thing you tell me to do, Dad—make a joke whenever you are nervous about anything."

Andy laughed. "So what did you say?" he asked.

"Well, I walked up to the front of the class and said, 'Hello everyone, my name is Franklin Fraser, and I'm a black boy," said Franklin.

Andy laughed; he held tightly to the chain on the swing and started to shake it.

"That was funny," said Andy. "Did they laugh?" he further asked Franklin.

"Yes, they all laughed, but not because it's funny, because it's derogatory to black people, and it was coming from a black boy," said Franklin.

"Are you sure you are nine, Franklin?" Andy jokingly asked.

"Well, Mom does teach me a lot," said Franklin.

"Speaking of Mom, she is probably making her way home now; let's go," said Andy. He checked his watch; it was 11:59 am.

Andy and Franklin walked off and came to the jungle gym, where the Mexican family was still standing. Franklin then realized the grandma was crying while the granddad was holding the little child, with light skin, long rich Spanish hair, wearing a Disney dress, with a wand in her hand.

"Why are you crying, ma'am?" young Franklin asked the Mexican grandma.

She looked at Franklin's chubby cheeks. "Oh, little one, they killed my son," she said.

"Franklin, mind your business," said Andy. "I'm sorry, ma'am, excuse my son," he further said.

"Badmen on bikes took daddy away," said the little girl as she ran to Franklin. "Hey, little boy, you want to play?" she asked. "Sure," said Franklin.

"No time for that, Frankie; Mommy is waiting for us," said Andy.

"I know you, Papi—you live at that yellow house up that hill. Don't you remember me?" the old man asked Andy.

"No," Andy replied.

"Well, we run the laundromat your wife washes at," he said.

"I see. Mr. Rodriguez," said Andy.

"Yes," he said.

"My condolences and I hope you find your son," said Andy as he walked off.

"Bye, little boy," said the little Mexican girl.

Upon walking away, Andy witnessed a man stopping by the Mexican couple, driving an unknown black vehicle. The man got out—he was a slim, muscular, built Mexican man in black pants, with a tight black shirt with the sleeves stretched widely from his big arm muscles; he had a short, faded haircut like Franklin's, chiseled facial features, and no beard no mustache. He made eye contact with Andy as he put the couple in the black-tinted-up car.

Andy got home and made his way in; Cedella was already in the shower. Franklin went back to watching cartoons—it was "Dragon Ball," he was excited to watch. Andy walked to the bathroom door. He knocked.

"Who is that?" Cedella asked.

"Hey, honey. I'm back, how are you? I miss you," he said.

"What!" said Cedella as she turned the shower off. "What did you say, honey?" she asked.

"Nothing, I was just saying we are home," he said.

Franklin then turned the TV up, thinking they were talking too loudly.

"You guys went to the park?" she asked.

"Yes," he said.

"Honey, why don't you come in the bathroom," said Cedella.

Andy opened the door; Cedella was getting out of the shower naked, drying her hair with the towel.

Cedella stood around 5 feet 8 inches, age 26, light skin, small afro hair, with a slim, attractive build, tiny waist, shaved vagina, big ass, smooth black skin without a blemish, and stiff breasts with stiff nipples.

She then turned to the mirror as she spoke.

"How was the park?" she asked.

As Andy looked at Cedella's big round ass as she continued to dry her hair, he walked up to her from behind, braced on her butt, dropped his weight on her, pushing her to the face basin. Andy got hard and quickly fingered his wife. She then used her big ass to push him off; Andy's dick was now hard as a rock in his pants.

"Franklin is sitting out in the living room, honey. Tonight after you come back from your show," said Cedella.

"Okay, babes," he said, "By the way, tonight's show is in Midtown; the owner of Shooters Pub hooked me up," said Andy.

Moments passed. It was now 6:30 pm in the afternoon. Franklin was fast asleep, and Cedella was sitting around the dinner table in her white see-through lingerie, drinking ginger mint tea.

Andy got ready for his first comedy show out of town. When he got to the place, the place was already packed with locals, ready to see young talents run their mouths. A few acts had already gone up before Andy; some of them got a few laughs, and some didn't. The crowd was getting bored and needed a change, then the announcer spoke.

"Ladies and gentlemen, please help me welcome Andy Fraser to the stage, all the way from King Town," said the announcer. Andy was backstage, pondering, thinking nonstop. Franklin's ideas ran through his mind, thinking to himself if he should try a kid's joke. Well, he did; Andy had decided to try his son's idea.

Moments later, and it was now Andy's turn to perform, he got up on stage, looked at the crowd, and he got a little nervous for some reason. This feeling had never happened to the young comedian since he had mastered his craft; it must be a new place. He then grabbed the corded mic and pushed the stool to the right of him.

"Hello, Midtown," he said. As he looked at the crowd, everyone looked on in silence; the crowd didn't react at all.

"Looks like Midtown is a Low town," he said.

"Boo!" said a man from the crowd. Andy couldn't see the person clearly, but he did make eye contact with the individual; in Andy's head, he was wondering to himself if it was now time to pull out the new type of joke he got from Franklin. He didn't hesitate.

"Hey, Midtown, let me tell you all a story. When I used to attend Elementary school in Chicago, I had a teacher named Mrs. Callaway. One day Mrs. Callaway asked us all to introduce ourselves and say something special as well, and there I was, sitting and hiding in the back, not wanting to be called upon, even holding my head down, and can you believe that bitch Callaway still called on me first?" he said.

The crowd chuckled a little, but not a full laugh.

"'Mr. Fraser, could you kindly step to the front of the class, introduce yourself, and tell us one thing special about yourself,' said Mrs. Callaway."

The crowd was now paying more attention to Andy.

"I then walked from the back of the class; you could see all the kids looking at me, nervous as hell, so I stepped to the front of the class, standing there in my blue jeans and Cosby sweater. Shaking and shivering, nervous as hell, I remember what my dad said to me; whenever you are nervous, just tell a joke about anything," said Andy.

The crowd is now pulling to the edge of their seats; Andy is grabbing the audience's attention at full.

"So, I stood there, and I said to the class, **'MY NAME IS ANDY FRASER, AND I'M A BLACK BOY.',**"

The crowd started laughing at a tremendous rate—nonstop laughing. Andy then switches to the other side of the stage, almost knocking the stool down.

"A lot of death in the news, recently. I ran into an old couple today telling me about their son going missing; very tragic," said Andy.

"AWW!" the crowd said in unison. Then Andy spoke again.

"Hey, Midtown, you see, when I die, I want to go to hell because I'm positively sure that is where Madonna is going, and I want a piece of that ass," he said.

The crowd chuckled. He continues.

"Full Gucci down with my rich black ass stepping through the gates of hell," said Andy. The audience started cracking up again; Andy was now on a winning streak, charming everyone down to their bones.

"A rich man in hell, hell yeah!" said someone in the crowd.

"Oh! Yes!" Andy replied. He then returned to the middle of the stage, grabbed the stool, sat on it, and quickly fixed the mic cord. The crowd was now waiting for him to speak again; he smirked. He knows he has them in the palm of his hands.

"Hey, Midtown, if I had all the money in the world, you know what I would do with it?" he asked the crowd.

"What?" one patron asked. Andy stared at him and smirked.

"I would buy us all condoms, so we can all fuck this world with protection before George does," said Andy.

You could hear the loud laughter as it started from the back of the pub. Everyone laughed their eyes out. Andy looked at the audience and smiled again.

"Fuck Bush!" someone from the crowd shouted.

"GOOD NIGHT, MIDTOWN! IT WAS PLEASURE BEING HERE," said Andy as he made his way backstage.

Andy was so captivating; he considered asking for another night.

Moments later, the owner of the pub was now paying Andy some money; he gave him $200. They shook hands, and the owner said thank you, but just before walking away, Andy asked a question.

"Is there any way I can work tomorrow again?" Andy asked the owner.

"I would love to, but the list is full for tomorrow," he said, "Are you available next weekend?" he further asked.

"Yes," he said.

Andy made his way outside.

Walking to his car, he couldn't wait to head back to King Town to tell Cedella about the good news.

Suddenly, someone came up to Andy—a man standing at 6 feet 2 inches, a big redneck guy, wearing a black hat, black leather biker jacket with no sleeves, and chains all over his black jean pants. Next to him was a long blonde-haired woman pale white skin, with a boney face, high cheekbones, big hoop earrings, and a skinny black leather jacket with the same skull and bone logo.

"Hey, you got skills, man. My name is Ace," he said.

"Thank you, Ace," said Andy.

"No problem, man. I will come see you again tomorrow," said Ace.

"What do you mean?" Andy asked.

"You are definitely on tomorrow," Ace replied.

"I would love to, but the owner said the list is full for tomorrow," said Andy.

"Don't you worry about what the owner said. Just show up, my man," said Ace as he patted Andy on the shoulder.

"You were the one who booed me earlier," said Andy.

Ace laughed and said, "Yeah, sorry, man. Me and my wife really loves comedy; our therapist said it's good for us," said Ace.

"Honey," said the blonde with a concerned look on her face.

"Oh, sorry, babes. This is my wife, Carla," he said.

Andy looked at Carla; Carla still had this look on her face of concern.

"See you tomorrow, my man," Ace further said. He then gave Andy a thousand dollars; Andy was so surprised he paused for a minute.

"Are you sure, man? This is a lot of money," he said.

"There is more where that came from," said Ace.

"Thank you, man," he said.

"No problem, I will be having all my buddies there also," said Ace as he got on his bike. Carla then climbed on with her flat butt—a nice shape, though. The exhaust from his Harley Davidson pulsated and smoked as he blasted off.

"Big guy," said Andy. He then walked to his car.

Andy made his way back to King Town in celebration. He got home, it was 10 pm, and Franklin was still in bed. Cedella was already naked in bed; Andy got in, trying not to make too much noise, took his jacket off, hung it up, loosened his tie, took his shoes and socks off, and neatly sneaked in bed and lay down. He then looked up at the ceiling and smiled. Cedella then took his arm and pulled it over her, pulling him closer to her; he got closer as he braced on his wife's big naked butt.

"How was it, babe?" she asked.

"I won big tonight, honey," said Andy.

She then turned around to face Andy, and he pulled out the $1200 from his pocket and gave it to his wife; she took it, holding it like a gambler.

"Where did you get this money from?" she asked Andy.

"Well, I made $200, but this biker guy gave me a big tip because of my new jokes and said he is bringing his biker buddies to come see me tomorrow," Andy told his wife.

"That is good, honey; what were your jokes?" she asked.

Andy ended up telling all the jokes to Cedella, and after she heard them, she couldn't stop laughing.

"Those are actually funny, but do you know why they laughed?" she asked.

"Because it was degrading to black people, and it was coming from a black person."

"Yes, how did you know that?" she asked.

"I know a lot," he said.

"What do you mean 'you know a lot'?" she asked as she smiled.

"Okay, honey; Franklin told me this joke," he said.

"What you mean Franklin told you this joke?" she asked as she put the money down on the bedside table. She then sat up straight. Andy sat up straight as well and told everything Franklin had told her at the park. Cedella couldn't stop laughing; then she spoke.

"But don't you think they are a little too personal and daring?" she asked.

"No, they are all about me," he said.

"And please keep it that way," She replied abruptly. He looked at her in silence; then Cedella lay back down.

Moments later, Andy and Cedella had missionary sex, trying to do it softly. After the sex and when Cedella had cum, she fell asleep. Andy pulled the cover over her, looked at his wife, then spoke. "Why would she say that?" he said to himself; as he watched her sleep, he then went to bed.

It was now Sunday morning, 8 am. Cold outside.

Franklin was already up watching cartoons, and Cedella was now getting up, making her way into the living room. She saw Franklin and walked over to him,

"Hey, Franklin honey, good morning," she said while she kissed him on the forehead.

"Good morning, Mom, and you need to brush before kissing me, Mom," he said.

Cedella looked at young Franklin like, "Boy, shut up," then went to the bathroom to brush her teeth. She quickly peeped into the room; Andy was talking to himself again.

"Honey, are you okay?" she asked.

"Yes, honey, just practicing some new jokes for tonight," he said.

Andy had lied—Andy was thinking about what his wife had said the night before, about keeping it personal, and decided not to tell his wife that he was planning to tell the same type of jokes, but this time he would pick on people from the audience.

Moments later, it was 6:30 pm. Andy had decided to take Cedella with him since she was off and hadn't been out in a while, leaving young Franklin by himself. Well, young Franklin had already proven to be a very responsible kid, so they never worried.

The couple was getting ready to leave, Andy putting his jacket on, Cedella tying her scarf, dressed in a short white dress, with a white blouse, black jacket, and black heels.

"You are beautiful, Mom," said Franklin as he sat on the couch.

"Thank you, son," she replied.

"Hey, Dad, I have another joke for you," he said.

"Go ahead, son," said Andy.

"Honey, we are already late," said Cedella.

"It's fine, babe; tell me the joke, Franklin," he said.

"Why is my hair so short?" he asked Andy.

"Why?" he asked.

"Because I go to the barber, not the gardener," he said.

The joke was so sudden, Cedella started cracking up first, then Andy started laughing as well.

"You get it, Dad?" he asks his dad.

"Yes, I get it. If it was the gardener, your hair would be tall," he continued. He then smirked.

"Good one, son," said Cedella.

"You should say that one tonight, Dad," he said.

"Sure, son," said Andy.

Andy and his wife made their way to the back of the house, where they had parked. While they were walking, someone shouted, "Mrs. Fraser, hold on."

They turned around; it was the Mexican man. "Mr. Rodriguez, how are you?" Cedella said. Moments later, she continued, "Did I leave something at the laundromat again?"

"Haha, not this time," said Mr. Rodriguez.

"I remember you," said Andy.

"I know; I was at your show last night. I heard you mention me and my wife; you are a funny man," said Mr. Rodriguez.

"Thank you," said Andy.

"But after the show, I saw you talking to a very bad guy. Please be careful," he said and walked off, leaving the Frasers confused.

"That was weird," said Cedella. "We are running late," she further said. They quickly rushed to the back of the house, got in the car, and drove off.

The Frasers were now making their way to Midtown, to the Crowbar Pub for round two, for the encore. Andy was excited to perform; they made it and parked at the front; both he and Cedella walked towards the back of the pub, where the owner had let them in. The place was already packed, with more people still buying tickets outside. Andy got in, and they got settled.

Cedella started counseling Andy, "Hey, remember, to keep it personal," she said as a reminder.

"Yes, honey, don't worry," he said. Then suddenly, the announcer spoke.

"Ladies and gentlemen, last night was so spectacular, we had to bring him back, thanks to my man Ace," he said. "Ladies and gentlemen, please help me welcome Andy "Mr. Charming," Fraser to the stage." The audience was ignited by the announcement. Andy then entered from the left side; leaving his wife standing at the curtains, he made his way on stage.

The crowd was in full support of Andy; they cheered very loudly,

"Andy! Andy! Andy!" the crowd cheered for him; on and on, they chanted. Andy looked at the front row; the entire front row was strictly a White, redneck biker gang, both men and women, all dressed in black leather jackets, with scary ass tattoos and chains—about 10 of them, all with their wives. Ace spoke.

"Give it up for my man Andy," he said while looking at Andy. He smiled, and he sat back down.

Andy was now ready to perform; he put his water bottle on the stool, took the corded mic out of the stand, looked in the crowd, and said, "HELLO, MIDTOWN."

The crowd got wild—nonstop cheering; Andy then stretched out both hands and waved, telling the crowd to settle down. The crowd quieted down. Andy then pointed to the crowd, and he pointed to someone from the back.

"Hey man, what is your name?" said Andy.

"Who, me?" said the guy in the crowd from the extreme back.

"Yes, you. Who else, man?" said Andy.

"Mark," he said.

"Is that your wife, Mark?" Andy asked.

"Yessir," he said.

"Do you know why your wife runs with every argument she hears?" he asked.

"No, why?" Mark asked.

"Because women are the quarterbacks of conversations." The crowd laughed hard, the bikers in the front cracking up. Andy's new and improved jokes seemed to be killing it. He then walked more to the front of the stage and pointed at Mark's wife.

"How about you, madam? Do you know why your husband does long hours at work?" he asked Mark's wife. She laughed and asked, "No, why?" as she looked at Mark.

"Because he only does two minutes at home," said Andy, while he made a circle with his thumb and index finger, using the mic as a dick to indicate he was talking about sex.

Andy's wife saw this and started laughing hard; the crowd was laughing hard. Andy then walked to the left of the stage and raised his two hands again, signaling to the crowd to calm down. He looked at Ace. Andy then made eye contact with Ace, he said.

"My man, Ace," said Andy.

"Yes, sir," said Ace as he laughed passionately with Andy.

"Everyone, give it up for Ace," said Andy. The crowd then cheered with beers in their hands.

Ace then raised his hands and spun a few times. Then sat back down.

"Hey, Carla," said Andy; Carla was smiling with Andy as she spoke.

"Hey, Andy," she said. Ace looked at them and laughed. Andy then turned his attention back to Ace.

"Ace, do you know why your Carla's pussy hair is so tall?" said Andy.

Ace giggled, "Because she didn't cut it," said Ace. The crowd chuckled as they waited for Andy's comeback.

"No, because she is seeing the gardener and not the barber." The crowd went nuts, everyone rolling out of their seats and laughing hard— except the redneck biker gang. Ace looked at Carla; Carla looked at Ace. Andy was enjoying the crowd's passionate response. Ace looked at Cedella in the left corner, then looked at Andy. Andy saw Ace's face, and he realized Ace was pissed because he and his guys were the only ones not laughing. Andy decided to wrap up the show. He then stepped back to the middle of the stage.

"Thank you, Midtown, and have a safe drive home," said Andy.

He then put the mic back in its stand and took the water bottle up, Ace and the others still sitting staring at him. With the most cynical look, he walked off, grabbed his wife's hand, and they went back to the dressing room.

Andy was now collecting his payment,

"Here you go, Andy," said the owner of Crowbar Pub. He handed Andy $7,000. Andy looked at Cedella; Cedella looked at the package.

"What is this?" Andy asked.

"Well, Ace said if all your jokes hit, I should pay you $7,000, and you did it, man," said the owner.

"WHO IS THIS ACE GUY?" Cedella asked.

"I have to go now; you guys get home safe," said the owner with a scared look on his face as he walked off in a hurry.

Andy and Cedella were now making their way out. Upon walking, something seemed to be worrying Cedella, and she spoke.

"I don't think he liked that joke," she said to Andy.

"It's just a joke, babe," said Andy.

"Babes, I told you to keep the jokes on you," said Cedella.

"Cedella, stop the worrying; everything is okay," he said.

Moments later, everything was now closed; Andy and his wife were making their way to the front parking lot, only to see a full biker gang leaning on their car, waiting for them. Andy kept walking with no fear. He then got to his car.

"Can you get out of my car, please?" said Andy as they ignored him and stared at him weirdly.

Then Ace shouted. "Hey, Andy, my man, can I have a word with you?" said Ace as he approached from the right of Andy. Cedella was holding Andy's hand very tight and a little scared.

"Sure," said Andy. He walked over.

"Do you know me?" Ace asked.

Andy looked all confused. "What do you mean? I met you last night," said Andy.

"Okay, do you know my wife," he asked.

"What is this?" Andy asked.

"How the Fuck did you know about my wife's affair?" he asked.

Andy stood there in confusion. "What are you talking about, my brother?" he asked.

"I'm not your fucking brother," he said. "You direct a joke to me and my wife; that wasn't cool, asshole," he said.

"But I made a joke about everyone," he said.

"Do I fucking look like everyone, Andy?" he replied.

Andy was still confused. Looking at his wife while he looked at the entire biker gang.

"What is going on, man?" he asked. Then Carla shouted out.

"I fuck the lawnmower, boy, okay? Can we fucking leave now?!" Carla said. She started crying.

"Ohh!" said Andy. "Listen, man; I don't know you or your wife. It was just a coincidental joke," he said.

"I'm not going back to that fucking therapist," said Carla as she walked off crying.

Ace then looked at Andy, "Watch your back, NIGGA!" he said and walked off.

"Let's go, boys," he said. They all jumped off the car and stared at Andy and Cedella as they passed them by.

Moments later, they all went their separate ways. Ace and his gang had ridden off, and Andy and Cedella were making their way home as well. It was a silent drive; no one spoke.

They made it home, and they got settled. Both Andy and Cedella were sitting around the dining table; the TV was still on; it was the late-night talk show. Andy looked at the TV in rage.

"Why does Franklin watch this stuff?" said Andy.

"Do you know who that is?" Cedella asked Andy.

"I told you, honey; I met him last night," said Andy.

"Not Ace, fool; I'm talking about the man on the talk show," she said.

"Who is he?" he asked.

"That is the local author, Andre Paul," she said.

"Who is that, honey?" he asked.

Then Franklin suddenly walked out of his room, rubbing his eyes, standing in his Batman pajamas.

"Dad, did you tell the joke," he asked.

"Yes, son," he said.

"Did you kill it?" he asked.

Andy laughed.

"Yes, son," said Cedella. Franklin then returned to bed.

It was now 11 p.m.; the Frasers were now trying to forget what had happened in Midtown, so they went to bed.

Sound asleep. 2:00 a.m.

A loud bang! came from the front door. Andy jumped up; Cedella was still asleep. Andy got up, grabbed his baseball bat, walked to the front door, and looked through the window. What he saw was so frightening he stepped back and had to look again. When he looked, he saw around 20 bikers—just males, with white ghost masks and long ropes wrapped up in cowboy style. Twenty Harley Davidsons motorcycles were parked in unison in front of Andy's house, and to the side was a black minivan. Then, all of a sudden, five of the bikers started to approach the house. Andy got scared and quickly rushed to Franklin's room.

"Franklin, wake up, son; we have to go," he said. Franklin was now stretching in confusion.

"Dad, what is going on?" he asked.

"Bad guys are coming to take us away," he said. The biker broke in.

"WHERE ARE YOU, NIGGA?" one biker said.

They started to trash the place. Cedella ran out of the room with her see-through lingerie, all frightened.

"What is going on?" she said as she turned the light on. She saw five bikers in white ghost masks.

"What the fuck are you doing in my fucking house?" she said.

"Where is your husband?" one biker asked.

Andy then came out, having left Franklin under the bed.

"What do you want?" Andy asked.

"That is up to our leader," he said.

"Who is your leader?" Cedella asked while one biker stared at her legs in her see-through lingerie.

"Yo, boss! Can I fuck his wife? She is very sexy," said the masked man who was standing close to Andy. Andy instantly got upset.

Cedella pulled her lingerie tighter,

"I'm calling the cops," she said and started to reach for the phone. One of the bikers slapped her in the face, and Cedella fell. Andy then jumped on the guy, pulled his mask off, and saw his face.

"I know you," he said. "Mark," he further said.

Then one biker knocked Andy out with a blunt object. Andy passed out.

Moments after waking up, Andy came to the realization that his wife and child were both tied up and gagged next to each other on the couch, with Andy bleeding from the head while his blurry vision recovered.

"Please don't do this. What do you want?" he asked.

Then suddenly, the front door opened; entering the chat was none other than Ace himself, making his way to the scene. Andy looked up at him; he was the only one not wearing a mask.

"Not so funny now, Mr. Funny man," said Ace. "Hahaha, looking who is laughing now," he further said.

"Ace, can I fuck his wife?" said Mark while he held his dick in his pants and looked at Cedella in her see-through lingerie. Then Ace spoke.

"YES, AFTER I FUCK HER," that was what Ace said.

"Hold her down and spread her legs," he further instructed. They grabbed her, and she screamed.

"Please don't do this," said Andy, crying nonstop and bleeding hard from the head.

Two of the bikers then held Cedella down on the couch, pulled her legs apart, ripped her lingerie off, and brought Franklin back to his room.

"Please, don't do this," said Andy, who was trying his hardest to get away.

Ace then dropped his pants and started to stroke his dick, but his dick was not standing up. He started to squeeze Cedella's big butt, but nothing. Moments after getting it up—it was only four inches of a dick—Ace started to fuck Cedella from the back, and she cried out. Andy couldn't watch; he turned away. They all fucked Cedella that night; they all rammed her from the back really hard.

Moments later, the bikers were leaving when Mark said. "Boss, they've seen your face and mine. What now?" Mark asked.

"Kill the woman and bring the kid with us," he said.

"And Andy?" he asked.

"Stay and watch him, do not kill him yet, let him suffer a little longer, let him think about all those white dicks in his wife and then kill him when you want," he said.

Mark then took a pillow, took his silencer gun out, put the pillow over Cedella's head, and gave her seven headshots. Andy fainted; the others took Franklin with them and tossed him in the back of the minivan. They then left the scene, leaving one bike outside.

A moment later, Mark was the only one at the house with Andy, waiting to kill him, when he got a call from Ace. He answered.

"Kill him now," said Ace. He hung up.

Mark then put his silencer to Andy's head. Pow! Pow! Pow! Three shots went off, and Andy fell to the floor.

Then suddenly, Mark fell to the floor as well. Mark fell right in front of Andy, with his eyes wide open, bleeding from his head, pupils dilating. Then a sudden footstep came into the house. A man walked over to Mark and shot him three more times in his head. Andy, scared as hell, looked up at the stranger and said, "Mr. Rodriguez?" before fainting.

Moments later, Andy woke up only to find himself untied on the couch; he started crying.

"They all raped my wife," he said as he cried immensely. "They took my son," he further said.

"I saw everything," said the guy, dressed in full black with a black felt hat.

"You are not Rodriguez, but I saw you that day when you picked them up in the black-tinted car," said Andy.

"So, what do I do now?" Andy asked.

"Who the fuck is this Ace guy?" he further asked.

"My name is Mario, and I need you to come with me," said Mario,

"Come where?" he asked.

"My dad's laundromat," he said.

Moments later, both men were now making their way to the laundromat. They went in; Mario then turned the light on—you could see all the washers and driers.

Andy stopped suddenly. "Please, can you tell me who this man is?" he asked.

"Okay, my brother was working undercover as a lawn caretaker at the White Ghost biker gang estate, but reports had stopped coming in from him; for like a month, we heard nothing, so we had believed he had gotten exposed and possibly gotten killed," he said.

"You see, I was at your show tonight, and it was your joke that gave me the lead I wanted," said Mario.

"It was a coincidental joke," he said with a somber tone.

"Coincidental or not, it helps," said Mario.

"At what fucking cost," Andy shouted.

"I didn't mean it like that," said Mario.

"Please come with me; we have work to do," he said. They both walked to the back. Mario opened a secret door; they went in and walked down a long stair leading to something like a basement. Mario turned the light on, and one by one, the lights came on. Both left and right sides had shelves with various types of weapons, and on the wall were over 50 different photos with faces of the White Ghost biker gang. Mario looked at Andy; Andy looked at Mario. Then looks at Ace's picture. He then suddenly got angry. Mario spoke:

"READY TO GO GET YOUR SON AND KILL THESE MOTHERFUCKING REDNECK BASTARDS?"

[THE ROAMING BISON]

Lennord County: a place of wooded areas, barns, farm animals, and a whole lot of untold mysteries. Summers in Lennord County are always bright and sunny; most, if not all, days are piping hot, and the heat from the sun fluctuates between 75 to 98 degrees. The towns are always full of shoppers, rich in diversity, with all types of people from all over enjoying what each town has to offer.

The county is known for a lot of scenic back roads, roads that give off a type of creepy, somber feeling; I'm talking about feelings of haunted landscapes, with quaint villages, graveyards, and houses that look like churches. The locals of the county consider this a blessing, for Halloween is the county's most celebrated festivity. Guess that is why it's called the county of untold mysteries.

It was June 1995.

Kewayne Matthews, now on summer break and ready to work his favorite summer job, was a black teenage boy who recently turned 17, standing six feet tall, with a skinny body and nappy hair he hardly combs. The teen could always be seen wearing Adidas hooded sweaters with sweatpants to match—well, that is when he was not dressed in his Stewart's uniform. Kewayne enjoyed smoking pot and grouping music reggae music—the teenager strictly listened to Bob Marley and Peter Tosh. Kewayne lived in Midtown with his dad, Carlton Matthews, who was the manager for four different Stewart's shops, thus making him a busy man.

Carlton, 6-feet 1-inch tall, nappy hair as well, with a very sharp edged-up, clean cut beard, black mustache, slim athletic body type, with a chiseled jawline, black eyes, dark skin, always dressed in black suits with a Stewart's logo on the pocket. He graduated from NEPA University with a B.S. in Business Management. Carlton is freshly divorced—his wife left him due to religious beliefs; you see, Carlton was an atheist, while his wife Sindy followed the blood of Christ.

Because of the breakup, and the move-out, Kewayne was forced to choose between his parents; obviously, he chose his dad. "All of Kewayne's friends live in Lennord County, so it's unnatural to take him from this environment," his dad often said. Most weekends, Kewayne would visit his mom in Bridgeport, Connecticut, which is about a two-hour drive from Lennord County.

Kewayne had been driving since age 15 and got his license and first car at 16. His dad spoiled him, the reason was that Carlton tried hard to compete with his ex-wife, but despite all of that indulgence, Kewayne and Carlton had a great father–son relationship. Now we really see why he chose to live with his dad.

Let me be honest with you: the real reason why Kewayne did not go with his mom is not because of his friends or anything like that. Would you believe this 17-year-old boy passionately enjoyed the back roads of Midtown and said, "It gives me a great deal of peace,"? For him, it was all about the country scenes, reggae music, and his weed, as he said, "It's the medication for the meditation."

It was a Saturday, the first weekend since Lennord County High School began its summer break. Carlton and Kewayne are both staying home.

A big two-story house, painted in grey and white—the house was located on the outskirts of Midtown, in a gated community, with five bedrooms, all white inside, with a big passageway that separates four of the bedrooms, and at the end of the passageway was where you found the master bedroom. The kitchen, living room, and bathrooms were all upstairs.

It was 10 o'clock in the morning and 80 degrees already. Kewayne was stretching and waking up. He turned the air conditioner off and made his way to the kitchen. Kewayne was wearing his red/green/gold mesh marina that he neatly tucked into his black Adidas sweatpants. He climbed the stairs.

"Who put a kitchen on the upstairs of a house," he sarcastically said to himself.

"Did you say something, son?" said Carlton, who was already sitting at the table in his black tuxedo suit, getting ready to leave.

"Oh! Hey, Dad," said Kewayne.

"Good morning, man," said Carlton as he sipped his coffee.

"Good morning," said Kewayne.

"Hey, Dad, when do I start work?" Kewayne asked his dad.

"About that—I'm sending you to the branch in Sage Town this summer, and you start on Monday," he said. "Your new schedule is in my briefcase; I will give it to you in a minute," Carlton further said.

"Is something wrong with the Stewart's in Midtown?" he asked.

"No, it's only getting renovated," he said.

"Oh, okay," said Kewayne. Then a call came on his cell phone.

"It's mom; she wants me to come see her this weekend," said Kewayne.

"Are you going?" Carlton asked.

"Yes," said Kewayne as he answered his phone. "Hey, Mom," he said while he walked down the stairs, signaling to his dad that he would be right back.

Moments later, Kewayne was talking to his mom outside, standing barefoot on the welcome mat as he chatted, blocking his face from the sun. Carlton was making his way out; he opened the front door and fist-bumped Kewayne.

"I left the new work schedule on the table, and yes, they are all day shifts," he said while he chuckled. Kewayne laughed as well.

"Okay, see you later, Dad," said Kewayne. Carlton then walked off.

"Is that Carl?" Sindy asked.

"Yes, Mom," he said.

"Is he still ungodly?" she asked.

"Mom, just because Dad doesn't believe in God doesn't make him evil. You do know that, right?" Kewayne asked his mom.

"Is he corrupting you, my son?" she asked him. "I pray he finds his way to church," she further stated. Kewayne laughed.

"I'm serious; please don't listen to a word he says. Jesus is king, and that is what the bible said, not to praise any other God. Please, Kewayne, don't believe anything that man says," she said.

"Mom, to be honest, I don't know what to believe, but I do believe Bob and Peter, though," he said and laughed at his own joke.

"Okay, I will see you later—love you, baby," said Sindy.

"Okay, Mom," Kewayne replied.

"Please say it back," said Sindy.

"Mom!" Kewayne replied with a strenuous tone.

"Say it back, Kewayne Matthews!" she shouted.

"Okay, love you, Mom," said Kewayne.

"That is my boy; I will see you soon," she said, then hung up.

There he sat, alone at his house, grouping music, making his own mixtape. Upon doing so, Kewayne had decided to take a drive; he had decided to stroll by the Stewart's Coffee Shop in Sage Town just to see what it looked like. He hesitated not; he got in his car, drove off, and turned his music on. It was Peter Tosh. He then grabbed one of his rolled spliffs out of the glove compartment. He added fire to it; he puffed the smoke, exhaled, and sang along to the music. He got off Dolson Ave and chose to take (I-84) to exit ten, then merged on 9W.

9W—the only road that connects all four towns in Lennord County, Sage Town, King Town, Nepa Town, and Midtown. So, to get anywhere in the county, you need to jump on 9W, and to get out of the county itself, it's either I-84 or I-87, which ends up merging with 9W, depending on your direction.

Moments later, Kewayne pulled up to the Stewart's Coffee Shop in Sage Town; he looked at the street sign. It said to turn right for John Street and keep straight for Maine Street, which merged into 32. He turned right on John Street and parked on the right side, with the front of his car facing Maine Street. Next to the car was a big white Church.

Kewayne sat still in his car, looking at the Stewart's building.

"I like this location," he said to himself, smiling with the spliff between his fingers, one hand on the steering wheel, hoody slightly over his head.

Then, all of a sudden, one of the workers came out, a white female with a high bun hairstyle, covered by a black topless Stewart hat she was constantly pulling down. She was also wearing black pants, with a burgundy Stewart shirt with her sleeves folded under her armpit. She pulled out a cigarette, lit it, started smoking, then turned around, facing the window of the shop—Kewayne saw her butt.

"Hoo! Nice ass," the 17-year-old said to himself. She looked over, and Kewayne quickly looked away and drove off. He turned right on Maine Street and drove three-tenths of a mile down, looking left and right.

"Oh, they have a Dallas Wiener, too," he said to himself; he then merged onto 32.

"Best hotdogs ever, that pepper cheese," he said to himself, smiling.

After moments of driving, Kewayne came to the realization that he was not familiar with the road he was on; he drove down a little further, and he then came upon a sign that said to keep straight to merge on KINGS HIGHWAY.

He drove half a mile out, and in no time, Kewayne had fallen in love with Kings Highway; he quickly pulled over to make another spliff, and upon making his spliff, he looked to the right and realized 9W was the next street over, but is separated by a riverbank, he then turned his music on and drove off.

Kewayne was enjoying the drive on Kings Highway; the 17-year-old was loving all the scenery he was getting. He then came upon a farm, where he saw a herd of bison—it was an open farm, the house, and barns were way in the back, but the bison were very close to the main road, with only a brown wooden fence to keep them in. Kewayne was mesmerized by the bison, and he then drove off.

After a moment of driving, he came upon a sign that said, "Merge on to 9W to get to Midtown." He merged, and from there, he cruised all the way home.

Moments later, after Kewayne had gotten home, packed his bag, and was ready to head out to Connecticut for the weekend, He dialed his dad.

The phone rang; Carlton answered.

"Dad, I will be leaving now; I will see you tomorrow," he said.

"Okay, and please drive safe; they drive crazy up there in Bridgeport," he said.

He hung up, got in his car, and drove off again. Moments later, after arriving at his mother's house, young Kewayne was extremely tired and hungry. He greeted his mom, and they hugged. She kissed him and made him something to eat. He ate, and he went straight to bed. Kewayne slept the whole night into Sunday.

It was now Sunday morning; he got up, went to the kitchen, and saw a note on the kitchen counter.

"Hey, K., I'm off to church, breakfast is there, help yourself, I will be back in 2 hours," the note said.

Kewayne went to the kitchen and got himself some frosted flakes and milk. First, he warmed the milk up, then poured it on the cereal. He liked it like that, he often said.

Two hours later, Sindy got home. She got in the house, and Kewayne was sitting on the couch watching TV. She went and sat beside him in her long blue church dress with a black church hat to match her short black hair and dark skin. She placed the bible on the glass table in front of the TV, next to the baby Jesus figurine.

"How are you, Kewayne?" she asked.

"I'm okay," he said while sliding down the couch, trying not to sit too close to his mom.

"Did you start that job yet?" she asked.

"Dad said it starts tomorrow," he said.

"Okay, that is good. Well, at least he is good for something," she said. "Your dad is a very unfair man."

"Please, Mom, let us not talk about Dad right now," said Kewayne.

"Okay, and why not?" she asked. "Because," he said. "Because what?" she asked.

"Nothing, Mom, I just don't want to talk about Dad right now," he said.

"Okay, are you hungry?" she asked. "Yes," he said.

Moments later, Sindy had cooked up some steak with mashed potato, with Lemonade on the side; they both enjoyed a long dinner with some good talk.

Time passed, and it was now 4 pm in the afternoon, and Kewayne was getting ready to leave, packed and ready to go. He jumped in his car and put the music on low, his mom watching him from the doorway.

"Please drive safely, and call me when you get home. Love you, baby," she said.

"Love you, Mom," he said and sped off.

The young driver had made it home safe that evening, back in Lennord County, and back home, he called his mom to let her know, he got home safe. It was 8 pm the night, and Kewayne had decided to take an early sleep. Work started at 8 am in the morning and ran to 3 pm.

NEXT MORNING.

Monday morning came, and he drove to his first day at the job. The manager was already waiting for him.

"Good morning Mr. Matthews and welcome to Sage Town," said the manager. Slim white guy, in his 40s, with a low fade haircut, clean beard, and glasses, in a black polo and black slacks.

"Good morning, sir," he said.

"Come, let me introduce you to the staff that is working now," he said. The manager then walked over, put his hands around Kewayne's shoulders, and led him into the shop.

They got in, and the manager then introduced everyone.

"Derek, this is Kewayne Matthews, Carlton's son; please take care of him," he said.

"What's good, bro," said Derek, a 5 feet 6 inches tall, 19 years old, muscular white dude, skin fade haircut, holding his Stewarts shirt in his hand.

"I'm good," said Kewayne.

"Where is Khloe?" the manager asked.

"She is in the bathroom, sir; she will be right back," said Derek.

"Okay, I will be taking off now; you guys handle this. Good luck, Kewayne," said the manager.

He then left, leaving only Derek and Kewayne.

"Do you know how to use the cash register?" he asked.

"Yes, it's not my first time working at a Stewart's," he said.

"Alright, my man, so you can take on the cash register for now; I will be right back, going to put my shirt on," said Derek.

Two minutes later, Kewayne was now getting acquainted with the cash register when the chandelier on the door went off, and someone came in. Kewayne made eye contact; it was the same short girl Kewayne had seen a day go, the one that made him say, "Hoo! Nice ass." They introduced themselves.

"So, you must be the new guy," said Khloe; you could smell the menthol on her breath.

"Yes," he said.

"Okay, welcome to Sage Town. My name is Khloe," she said.

"I'm Kewayne," he replied.

She then walks through the mini door by the cash register, the same register where Kewayne was standing. She slightly bounces upon Kewayne.

"You smell like weed," she said. Kewayne started to smell his hoody sweater.

"I smoke too," she said. "Where is Derek?" she asked.

"Oh, he went to change his shirt. Said he will be right back," said Kewayne.

"You want to smoke after work?" she asked Kewayne.

"Sure, why not," he replied, as they both made eye contact.

Derek, now making his way back in, joined the conversation. They all got acquainted, and a friendship grew fast, and just like that, the month of June had come to an end; the three had gotten closer and had developed a good relationship. Kewayne started secretly to like Khloe, and Khloe secretly liked him.

Khloe started to spend time at Kewanye's house, where they smoked together all the time. No sex had happened yet, just sexy talk and life stories. Even so, Kewayne had yet to tell her about the drives he took after work on Kings Highway.

JULY 1995

It was 3:03 pm in the afternoon. Kewayne was working as usual, waiting to leave, so he could drive and enjoy the back roads of King Highway. Kewayne had bought a new camera and decided he was going to start taking pictures of nature. There he sat, waiting for another worker to relieve him. Unfortunately, the worker had called out, saying she was not feeling well, and for the first time in Kewayne's work history, he had to stay on a little longer. He then called his dad to let him know he was working late. The extra shift had tired young Kewayne out; customers were coming in and out. The orders were mostly iced coffee and ice cream.

Moments later, Kewayne, now making his way to his car, had closed the shop and everything and checked his watch; it said 11 pm at night.

"I can't believe this woman did this to me," he said as he walked to his car.

He left, and he was now driving home in his Honda Civic, blasting Bob Marley music, the "Redemption," song, while he smoked and got high, looking at the night skies.

"This place really looks different at night," he said.

Everything Kewayne used to see in the daytime, he was now seeing at night; he told himself he was just going to enjoy the night and think nothing of it. Reggae music was blasting, and weed smoke was all over the car as he danced. He was now coming up to where the farm was. He pulled up to the bison, and he slowed down close to the wooden fence. It was a full moon with thick fog, and he pulled over. Looking over the fence, Kewayne saw only the silhouette of the bison appearing one by one as the moon broke away from the cloud.

"Wicked," he said.

With the spliff in his mouth, the car still in gear, he held down the clutch and brake. He then took his Polaroid camera out, and just as he was about to take a picture, Kewayne suddenly witnessed all the eyes of the bison instantly turn to fire. The bison started to run towards the fence as if they were coming for Kewayne, and he got so scared he eased his foot off the clutch and brake in a panicky state, instantly pressing the gas pedal, and almost crashed into the tree over by Mount Marion cemetery.

Moments later, after getting home, he was telling his dad the story about the fire-eyed bison he saw.

"Hahaha, son. Don't tell your mother this; she will think I'm doing this to you," he said as he laughed some more.

"You don't believe me, dad?" Kewayne asked.

"Of course not. A Bison's eye doesn't just turn to fire. You were probably high off that marijuana. Yes, I know you smoke," said Carlton.

"Oh, you do?" he said.

"Yes, Kewayne, I just didn't say anything because the weed doesn't affect your diligence. You are not a lazy boy, you are a very productive kid, and I'm proud of you," he said.

"Thanks, Dad, that is nice coming from you, but I'm not lying though; those Bison's eyes did turn to fire," he said.

"Hahaha, okay, son. Just go to bed and get some sleep," he said.

NEXT MORNING.

Kewayne was telling the story to Khloe.

"Yo! Khloe, I'm telling you those bison's eyes turned into fire," said Kewayne.

"I'm pretty sure you were just high, Kewayne," said Khloe. "Who is putting eggnog in the freezer?"

"You sound like my dad," said Kewayne.

"You guys still talking about that Bison shit?" said Derek, who had decided to take on an extra shift.

"Okay, if you guys don't believe me, why don't you all come with me tonight, then?" said Kewayne.

"I'm down; I'm not doing anything later," said Derek, flexing his muscles for no fucking reason.

"Khloe, how about you?" asked Kewayne.

"Okay, but your shift ends soon. Are you going to wait for us?" she asked Kewayne.

"Yes, babe," said Kewayne.

"Babe? What's going on," said Derek. "You guys hooking up?" he asked.

"Shut up, Derek," said Khloe.

"Anyway, Kewayne, make sure you make like three spliffs," said Khloe.

Then the shopkeeper's bell on the door went off, and a customer came in. Kewayne was making his way out at the time. The customer walked and passed him. Kewayne held the door.

Upon walking outside, Kewayne stopped and stared at something across the street, like he saw a ghost or something. He stood there for a while and then walked off.

Moments later, Derek and Khloe were now closing, Kewayne already waiting for them. He parked on John Street, with his car facing Main Street. They closed, they got out, and Kewayne revved his car.

"Yo, let's go," he said, with a spliff between his fingers, one hand on the steering wheel, and his hoody slightly over his head.

"Hold on, KayKay," said Khloe.

"Alright, let's go," said Derek as he turned the final key.

They all got in, and Kewayne drove off and turned right on Maine Street, which merged into Route 32. Khloe was sitting in the back, Derek in the front, Kewayne lit a spliff, then passed it to Derek, but Derek didn't smoke, so he passed it to Khloe. Derek was drinking an Appleton rum he got from Kewayne, which he got from his dad's house. Kewayne turned the music on, pushed his cassette tape down, and a nice beat came on, and then the lyrics: *"Legalize it, don't criticize it, legalize it, and I will advertise it."*

"Who is that?" Derek asked Kewayne.

"It's Peter Tosh," said Khloe.

"Wow! Khloe, you love reggae too?" Derek asked her.

"Yes, but Kewayne plays this song all the time in the car," she said.

"Be honest. Are you guys fucking?" Derek asked.

"Bro, could you settle down," said Kewayne.

They were now merging onto Kings Highway. Spliff after spliff, Khloe and Kewayne were now high as a kite. Derek was kind of tipsy, then he stretched his hand to the back and suddenly started to touch Khloe's legs.

"Stop," said Khloe.

"Stop acting like that; I was just touching your legs," said Derek.

"You literally rubbed my calf Derek; please don't do that again," said Khloe.

Derek then grabbed her calf again.

"Bro, could you not fucking do that!" said Kewayne.

"I knew it. You guys like each other," he said. As Khloe pushed over to the driver's side, Derek then turned his attention to Kewayne. "You like Khloe, bro," he said. Then Kewayne switched the song while Derek was talking. The beat of the song was now building up; while Derek was laughing at Kewayne and Khloe, the song started playing.

"There is a natural mystic blowing through the air. If you listen carefully now, you will hear, this could be the first trumpet, might as well be the last, many more will have to suffer, many more will have to die, don't ask me why."

"Natural Mystic," by Bob Marley was playing. Kewayne turned it up.

They were now coming up to where the Bison were; they parked on the roadside close to the fence and looked over; they saw nothing.

"Where are the bison?" Derek asked.

"Just wait for it," he said while he pointed to the sky, at the clouds. They all looked up, and they saw a thick cloud moving away from the moon, and in an instant, the silhouette of the Bison started to appear. They were now staring at the herd of Bison in the moonlight.

"Wow!" said Derek while they all continued to stare, not moving—the Bison were still as a statue. "But you said their eyes were fire?" Khloe asked.

"They were," Kewayne replied. Kewayne checked his watch; it was12 pm

"Okay, anyway, they are creeping me out. Can we go now?" said Khloe.

"What are you talking about? Let us go over there," said Derek, still drinking his Appleton rum.

"Yeah, let's go," said Kewayne.

They all got out of the car and walked towards the fence. They all leaned on the fence, then, in an instant, all the Bison's eyes became fire. One by one, they changed, then, out of nowhere, the herd of Bison started to chase Kewayne and the others.

They got frightened, and they ran to the street. With no time to break up, Kewayne and his friends got run over by a Walmart tractor-trailer with blinking lights that was passing through the backroads of Kings Highway. All three were broken from head to toe, Khloe's skull was crushed to where her eyeballs came out of her head, and Derek's torso was scraped down his ribs. Kewayne's head was ripped right off his body. The driver of the trailer tractor did not stop at all; he went straight on ahead.

The night was still dark, and the surrounding neighbors seemed to be unaware that this had just taken place; it was four hours later before someone discovered the bodies and called 911.

Day broke, 6 o'clock in the morning, and the scene was now full of paramedics, police, journalists, and a couple of Lennord County locals. Coroners cleaned up the remains of the teenagers, for the bodies had been scooped up 2 hours earlier. On the scene were Detectives Jones and Johnson, two tall black baldheaded detectives, ages 45 and 47, dressed in suits, handling the crime scene, pacing and pondering, trying to figure out what happened; the identification of the teens wasn't clear yet.

"Jones, what you think happened here?" asked Johnson.

"This is a weird one," Jones replied.

"What do you mean?" Johnson asked.

"Well, the bodies of the teens are in the street, but closer to the fence, where those Bison are, the car is parked next to the fence, so I'm confused as to why they were in the street and not in their car," said Jones.

"They found drugs in the car; they could have been high and decided to party in the middle of the street," said Johnson.

"True, just one problem," said Jones.

"What?" Johnson asked.

"They are all wearing Stewart's uniforms," said Jones.

"And?" Johnson asked.

"That means they are responsible kids, even if they smoke weed," Jones said.

"I see what you are saying," Johnson replied.

Moments later, the identification of the teenagers was revealed. They found Kewayne's phone; the car was still on, and "No Woman No Cry," was playing.

"Turn that down," said Jones. The cop doing the search turned it off.

"I said turn it down, not turn it off—that is Bob, you don't turn Bob off, you turn Bob down," said Jones. The officer then turned it back on and turned it down.

Jones then searched Kewayne's phone. Then searched his camera, and he saw a couple of naked pics of Khloe's naked pussy and breasts.

Jones was still confused about what was happening. By now, the paramedics had left. Jones and Johnson were now getting ready to leave;

they got back in their car, and Jones was now slowly driving off when Johnson shouted.

"Jones, who is that?" he asked.

"Who?" Jones asked.

"That guy with that huge sign in his hand," said Johnson as they both watched a man walking down and through the middle of the Bison.

"Must be the owner of the farm," he said.

A short white guy, around 5 feet tall, wearing big glasses, with a receded hairline, looking like a complete nerd, acting all nonchalant like he wasn't aware of the accident. He walked to the fence, climbed over, then started to nail the sign on the fence. He then got back over the fence and went straight back to his house.

"He is definitely the owner of the place; we will come back later," said Jones.

They drove off. Jones had decided to swing by the Stewart's Shop in Sage Town and recover the security footage of last night to see if he could gather any clues.

Moments later, Jones and Johnson got back to the station, and the families of the teenage victims were already present at the station. The LCNS newsgroup was milking the situation. "The Daily Lemon is probably going to milk this one," said Johnson to himself.

"Yes, just more scary stories for him to write about," said Johnson.

"Who?" Jones asked.

"Andre Paul," said Johnson.

"Who is Andre Paul?" Jones asked.

"It's all ready now, sir," said one officer, who was making his way to Jones

"What is ready?" Johnson asked.

"THE TAPE," he said.

Moments later, Jones and Johnson were now watching the security footage.

Both Jones and Johnson saw Kewayne stepping out of the shop and holding the door for a man. Then Kewayne stopped and paused and looked at a big Walmart tractor-trailer truck with the front lights going on and off, and then he walked off.

"That is our guy," said Jones as he wrote the license plate number down.

"What do you mean?" Johnson asked.

"You don't get it," said Jones

"No, I don't," he said.

"The kids couldn't see the truck because the light of the truck was not working properly," said Jones.

"So, you are saying the kids got run over when his truck lights went out?" Johnson asked.

"Precisely," said Jones.

"I know now that it's a hit and run, but something is bugging me about this whole thing," said Jones.

"What?" Johnson asked.

"Why did they run to the street?" he asked.

"You want to go back to the scene?" asked Johnson. "Yes," he said.

Moments later, the detectives drove back to the scene of the tragic incident. While cruising on Kings Highway, Johnson was enjoying the view.

"These back roads are so peaceful; I can't see no one dying here," said Johnson. Jones stares at him with a somber look.

They now pulled up to the scene again. They got out of the car, both looking around again.

"So, what you think, Jones?" Johnson asked.

"I think something forced them to run to the street," he said.

"Okay, but there is nothing around these parts but trees and those Bison," said Johnson.

And as soon as Johnson said bison, Jones walked down to where the guy had put the big sign, walking fast.

"What is it, Jones?" Johnson asked him, and Jones kept walking. He finally got to the sign, and he was looking at the sign, reading the sign.

"Come read this," he said to Johnson. Johnson was now walking fast to see what was inscribed on the sign. He finally got to Jones, stood beside Jones, he started to read the sign, which said:

"THESE BISON ARE NOT REAL. THEY ARE MECHANICAL BISON JUST FOR SHOW. BISON CAN BE SEEN MOVING IN A RUNNING MOTION. EYES TURN TO FIRE AT MIDNIGHT."

[THE URGE]

And lead us not into temptation but deliver us from evil: For thine is the kingdom, and the power, and the glory, forever. Amen. —Matthew 6:13

Sometimes, it's when you hide your fears that you become your fears; why not just face them? Why not just go to war with your fears and never come back until you win? Why not?

Selena was 21, of Greek descent, with fair skin, straight black hair, and hazel eyes, weighed about 130 pounds, had very bad asthma, never left her asthma inhaler; Selena never had sex, never had a kiss, never had a boyfriend; never even experienced the internet; she was homeschooled, her extra activities were just from home to church and church to home. Selena was of the Orthodox tradition, raised under strict Christian rules, following the no sex unless you get married commandment. Selena lived in Buffalo, New York, with her mom and uncle; her dad had passed away due to a very bad seizure. It was August 1997.

Church was in session, congregation full, with just white people, pastor already on the altar running his mouth about Jesus and God.

"Hear me, my people, for God so loved the world, he gave his only begotten son to die for our sins; say amen," said pastor Shepherd.

"AMEN!" said the congregation while they fanned themselves due to the 80-degree heat outside.

Selena was sitting in the second row, next to her mom, listening keenly to the pastor as he continued to preach.

"I know it's hot in here, but the Lord will provide," he said. Selena laughed and looked at her mom.

"Enjoying the words of the Lord, I see," said Iris, Selena's mom.

She stood 5 feet 7 inches tall, had a slim body, black hair, and hazel eyes, and was always seen wearing white church dresses with flower patterns on the shoulder and sleeves. Iris was a very caring mom, but she was also strict as hell. She restricted Selena from a lot of activities, which was taking away the young lady's adulthood. Iris had noticed this, and because Selena was now 21, she was thinking of ways to give her a little more freedom.

"Yes, every word," she replied.

Her mom then smiled at her, and the pastor continued to preach. Minutes later, Selena started to scratch her left cheek, immensely she scratched, making her face red.

"Stop, your face is going to start bleeding," said Iris, "Selena, stop!" Iris further said.

"But it itches, Mom," said Selena under her breath.

"I know, but church is almost over," said Iris.

"Okay, Mom," she said and quickly put her hands to the side.

They then reverted their attention back to the pastor.

"And my people, it has come down to that time. I will be sending the offering basket around," said pastor Shepherd.

Then a man stepped down from the church stage and started to collect offerings; he did the first row and now on to the second row,

"Offering today, ma'am?" he asked Selena.

"I have no money," said Selena, then he looked at Selena's red cheeks; he then went over to Iris.

"Offerings today, ma'am?" he asked. Iris then put $20 in the basket.

"Thank you, ma'am," he said.

"You are welcome," Iris replied.

Moments later, the offering collection came to an end, the congregation was dismissed, and everyone was now leaving; the last to leave was Iris and Selena.

As they were leaving, someone stopped them.

"Hey, Ms. Demakis, wait up," the offering man shouted as he quickly walked down to Iris and Selena.

"How may I help you, brother Vykis," asked Iris.

"I notice Selena has this rash on her face. My wife sells face products; she may have something for it," said Mr. Vykis, a short, frail white man, age 56, with a bald head and chubby body.

"Thank you, brother Vykis, but I will pass," she said and walked off. Iris and Selena then stepped through the big church doors.

"Hold on, Ms. Demakis, here is my wife's card. Think about it," he said. She took it, and she looked at it. Mr. Vykis then walked away.

"I don't even own a phone," she said. Selena laughed.

Moments later, Iris and Selena were now getting home. Selena went to her room, got in her bed without even changing her church clothes, and Iris walked in.

"Hey, Sel, are you okay?" she asked Selena. "No, Mom," she replied.

"Is it your face?" Iris asked.

"No, Mom," she replied.

"What is wrong?" Iris asked.

"Mommy, I feel so stuck, I feel restrained, I feel like there is so much I haven't seen, I feel like I'm stuck in one mindset, I feel like I'm not free, and I feel like my life has no purpose," said Selena.

Iris looked at her and shook her head. "Oh, Selena," she said under her breath.

"Okay, I have decided to send you to your aunt for the rest of the summer," said Iris.

"Aunty Mary," said Selena with a big smile.

"I knew that would make you smile," said Iris.

And just like that, Iris had decided to send Selena to Poughkeepsie, New York; Selena was delighted to go; a change of scenery might be the trick for her.

It was August 1997.

Packed and ready to go, Selena stuffed everything in one suitcase and now waited patiently on her uncle, who was taking her to the train station.

"Honey, make sure you don't forget your inhaler pump," Iris said.

"Yes, Mom, I have it," Selena replied. HONK! HONK! That was David blowing his horn.

"Uncle is here," said Selena.

She looked out the window; David had parked on the street but remained in the car. She then quickly went outside and ran to the car. Surprisingly, the wife of Mr. Vykis was already en route to Iris's house, stepping hard on Iris's grass; with a green bag in her right hand; it seemed like she had come to visit her. She passed Selena.

"Hey Sel, is your mom home?" asked Mrs. Vykis.

Tahlia Vykis was a 45-year-old white woman, standing at 5 feet 4 inches, with short black hair and blue eyes. She kept her body in good shape and wore tight-fitted clothing, even in church.

"Yes, she is," Selena replied.

"Are you leaving for somewhere?" Tahlia asked Selena.

"Yes, going to Poughkeepsie for the summer," she replied.

"Poughkeepsie, huh? Please be careful; there is this crazy guy named Kendall Francois who is killing only women. It is all over the internet," she said.

"Oh, I never watched the internet before," Selena replied.

"Okay, just be careful, my dear," she said.

"Thank you, Mrs. Vykis," said Selena as she made her way to the car. David then came out, grabbed her suitcase, and put it in the trunk. Then she went in, and David slammed the trunk.

"Hi, uncle," she said.

"Hey, Selena, how are you?" David asked.

"I'm good," she said as they watched Mrs. Vykis making her way to the house.

She knocked on the door. Iris then opened the door.

"Hey, sister Demakis, how are you today?" Tahlia asked.

"Where did you come from?" Iris asked.

"Oh, I was in the neighborhood," said Tahlia.

"Oh, I could've sworn you were just coming out of my brother's car?" she asked.

"Oh no, he was outside when I pulled up," Tahlia said.

"Okay, but why are you here?" she asked, as she peeped at Selena and David, who were about to leave soon.

"So, my husband was telling me you may be in need of some facial cream for Selena," she said.

"I already told your husband no," Iris said. Then she tried to close the door, then Tahlia blocked it with her leg.

"Can I come in?" Tahlia asked. And without hesitation, she forced her way in, and went straight to the dining table, then pulled out several face products from the green bag, displayed them to Iris, and lined them up on the table.

"This one right here will get rid of any rash and blemishes," she said. "And this here is called a Vicks VapoRub. This one can be applied to any affected area of the body. This one even gets rid of any bad asthma cough. Just keep it refrigerated after opening," said Tahlia, with Iris standing there, being nonchalant about the entire presentation. Then suddenly, she looked at the fridge top.

"HER INHALER!" Iris shouted.

"What?" Tahlia asked.

"Selena forgot her inhaler," she said while she stared at the pump on the top of the fridge.

"She said she had it; that girl is something else," she further said.

"Selena forgot her pump?" Tahlia asked again, even though Iris had just told her.

"Yes," she said with a serious voice. "She has to get her pump; she won't survive without it," said Iris as she panicked.

"Calm down, sister, just call David," said Tahlia.

"I don't have a phone; can you call him for me?" she asked Tahlia.

"Sorry, I left my phone at the house," she replied.

"Okay, I need to go to the payphone by the post office," said Iris.

She then rushed to her bedroom, put her brown cardigan on, and quickly rushed out the door.

Moments later, Iris was now outside, and Tahlia was leaving as well; they both were standing outside when Tahlia received a call. Her phone was ringing in her green product bag; it was a "Backstreet Boys," ringtone. Iris looked at Tahlia.

"I thought you didn't have a phone," Iris said.

"I'm sorry, I didn't know I had it," Tahlia replied as she giggled. Iris looked at her with a stern face.

"So, call David then," said Iris.

Tahlia then looked at her phone to see who was calling. It said David Demakis with an "SG," beside his name.

She immediately hung the call up and quickly deleted his name from contacts. After taking too long, Iris got impatient.

"Can I have the call or not?" Iris asked.

"Yes, just one second," she replied as she finished deleting the number.

"Yes, let me have the number," Tahlia asked Iris. Iris sighed.

"716-765-0000," she said. Tahlia then dialed the number. She gave the phone to Iris; Iris took the phone and put it to her face as it rang.

"Not to laugh," said Tahlia, "But the speaker needs to go to ears, not to your mouth, and the mic goes to your mouth, not to your ears," she further said as she cracked up.

David answered, "Hey, babes, why did you hang up," he said.

"I can't hear anything," said Iris as she acted confused.

"Well, you need to turn the phone around, Iris," said Tahlia. Tahlia then stepped towards her to assist her.

"I got it," she said.

Iris then turned the phone around. David now heard his sister's voice.

"Sister, is that you?" David asked.

"Hey David, I just borrowed Tahlia's cellphone to call you. How far are you?" she asked.

"I'm 5 minutes away from the station; what is wrong?" he asked.

"Okay, Selena forgot to take her inhaler with her," she replied.

"Oh no," said David. He then looked at Selena with a concerned face.

"What is wrong, uncle?" Selena asked.

"You forgot your pump," said David.

"Oh, I will be fine; my asthma only acts up when I get excited about something," she said.

"Sis! Selena said she will be fine, but don't worry, we will figure something out when I get back," he said.

"Okay, brother, see you later," said Iris.

"Okay, bye," David replied, then hung up.

"Your mom is very protective of you. I bet she is going to want to take the pump down herself," he said. They both laughed.

Several hours later, Selena was now boarding the Buffalo Amtrak, which would take almost seven hours to get there; she hugged and kissed her uncle, then told him bye.

"Have a safe travel, my dear, and don't do anything I wouldn't do," he said.

"Like what? Liking Mr. Vykis's wife?" she said. David looked at her and laughed.

"We are just friends," he said. Selena laughed and gave her uncle a final goodbye.

"Goodbye, uncle, see you in a couple of months," she said.

She then boarded the train.

Several hours passed, and Selena was now arriving at the Poughkeepsie Train Station; she walked, for her auntie's house was just 12 minutes away on foot. "20 Garden Street."

Upon arrival, Selena saw two U-Haul trucks packed with stuff, ready to go. She saw her aunt talking to one of the drivers. She then walked over; her aunt then looked around and saw her.

"Hey, Sel," said Aunt Mary with a wide smile; she was happy to see her niece.

Mary Demakis, standing at 5 feet 6 inches, age 45, blonde hair, sexy physique, boney face, high cheekbones, dressed like a fashion designer, who mostly wears black. Mary is the manager of a clothing store in

Woodbury Commons, where she sells her own designer clothing, and she is the total opposite of Iris.

"Hi, Aunt Mary," said Selena as she fluffed her long church frock that stretched all the way to her ankle.

"Aunt Mary, what is happening?" she asked.

"Oh! We are moving to a new home," said Mary

"Where?" Selena asked.

"A place called Lennord County," said Mary.

"Where is that?" she asked.

"Just another county over, takes about 40 minutes' drive," said Mary.

"Good, I don't want to be near that Kendall Francois guy," said Selena, with an innocent voice.

"You are not a prostitute, my child," said Mary as she laughed. "And by the way, we need to get you some new clothes, too," she further said.

"Okay," said Selena. She smiled. Mary then walked over and hugged Selena.

"I'm so happy to see you," she said. She then released her.

"Put your suitcase in my car," she said.

Moments later, Selena, her aunt, and both U-Haul trucks had left the Garden Street home, already crossed the Poughkeepsie Bridge, and were now cruising on 9W, making their way to Lennord County, taking in all the wooded areas of the county, all the farms, and farm animals.

"I heard this place has a lot of untold mysteries," said Mary.

"That is cool; I love mysteries," said Selena as Mary accelerated her way to her new home.

They finally arrived at the bridge-tunnel, Selena keenly staring at the big Lennord Junior Town Statue. She then looked at the Saint Monica Hotel next to it, and after that, she saw a sign that said,

"WELCOME TO SAGE TOWN,"

They then turned on Partition Street, Mary in front, while the two U-Haul trucks followed behind; they were now coming up to the first stop light, with a sign that said to turn right or left for Maine Street and keep straight for Partition Street. They drove past Maine Street, continuing Partition Street. They arrived; it was 204 Partition; it was still daytime, 75 degrees out. They all got out; Mary and Selena were now making their way in while the U-Haul drivers carried all the boxes from the trucks to the house.

"Nice house, Aunty," said Selena.

"Yes, it is. Ready to fix it up?" she asked.

"Yes," she replied with a smile.

"Well, I hope we have great neighbors, and not like Francois," Mary said ironically, then laughed at Selena.

To the left of the house was a brick house, which was occupied by an older couple, maybe in their 40s; to the right was a yellow house, occupied by an Italian man who was constantly not home.

Mary and Selena now got settled, boxes everywhere; the U-Haul trucks had left. Mary decided to unpack in the morning.

"Sel, I will be heading to bed soon, okay," she said, "Pick any room you want; the beds are already spread," she further said.

"Okay, Aunty," said Selena as she ran upstairs.

Mary then went to bed. She took the room closest to the street, while Selena took a room that was adjacent to the neighbor's kitchen.

"Bricks are so cool," she said to herself as she stared into the neighbor's house.

That night, now settled, Selena was relaxing in her bed but couldn't sleep. Eyes wide open, she got up and went to open the window. She then saw the neighbors fucking on the kitchen counter. She was startled, she pulled back, she then took another look, she pulled the curtain over her face, she peeped again, she saw the guy stroking the woman aggressively from the back, while the woman moaned, then bit her lips. Then something happened: Selena started to bite her lips as well. Then a certain liquid started running down her leg. She quickly looked to see what it was; she realized that she was leaking from between her legs. She quickly wiped and then came to the realization she was leaking from her vagina. Her clit started to jump, and she felt a strong tense feeling within the walls of her vagina. She grabbed her breast and squeezed really hard while the neighbors continued to fuck on the kitchen counter. Selena caught herself; she immediately stopped, grabbed her bible, and started praying.

"Sorry, lord, please forgive me for being led into temptation," Selena said.

She then went to the bathroom to wash her face, changed into her nightwear, then went back to her room. She closed the curtain and went to bed.

NEXT MORNING.

Selena woke up thinking about the hardcore sex she had witnessed, but what had stuck in her mind the most was the man slapping the woman's ass as she bit her lips.

"What am I doing?" she said to herself as she got dressed. Mary then called out for her.

"Sel, honey, come downstairs for breakfast," said Mary.

"Coming, aunty," she said as she made her way down.

She then went to the kitchen. Mary was at the stove.

"Good morning, Aunty," she said.

"Good morning, baby," Mary replied. She then turned around, with eggs and bacon in her hands, and handed it to her. She then took a glance at Selena's church clothing. She then laughed.

"You need some new clothes," she said.

Suddenly the doorbell rang; Mary then put the eggs down and quickly went to the door; it was the neighbors. They came over—a Spanish couple, a dark skin woman with tall black hair, dressed in pum-pum shorts and a spaghetti strap blouse, and a man with a bald head and dark skin, dressed in a beach shirt and slacks. Selena then went behind Mary to see who it was. They greeted Mary while she stood behind them.

"Hi, I realize you are new to the neighborhood, so we are just saying hi. My name is Alejandro, and this is my wife, Francesca," said Alejandro.

"Okay, I'm Mary, and this is my niece, Selena. She is from Buffalo and is here for the summer," said Mary.

"I see," said Alejandro. Francesca then handed Mary the cake she had brought.

"You can bring the pan back when you get the chance and enjoy the stay," said Alejandro.

The couple then left. While walking away, Alejandra gazed at Selena in her tall church frock. Selena saw this and looked away with a blush. No one else picked it up.

Mary then closed the door and went back to eating breakfast; Selena sat down as well.

"Sel, baby, when you finish eating, go find the boxes that say, "New arrival, size small," said Mary.

"Okay, Aunty," she said.

Moments later, after finishing breakfast, Selena went to fetch the boxes; she then brought them back to Mary and sat them down in front of her.

"Open them up," said Mary. She did so, the first box had only jeans, and the second box was different color blouses.

"Pick what you like and try them on," said Mary. "Okay, Aunty," she said. She smiled.

She went, and she tried them all. She then came back out in tight blue jeans and a pink spaghetti-strap blouse.

"Omg, you are sexy," said Mary. "You should come work for me at the store," said Mary while she laughed. "But I know your mom won't ever allow that to happen," she further said.

"Thank you, Aunt Mary. Can I keep them?" she asked.

"They are all yours, baby," said Mary. Selena was so happy she kept it on the whole day.

And just like that, the day came to an end. It was now 11 at night.

While resting in bed in her tight blue jeans and pink spaghetti strap blouse, she was pulling on the blouse string as she thought. Selena had decided to take a peek at the neighbors' kitchen. She looked for the first time, but she saw nothing, so she went to bed. After about five hours of sleep, and now 4 am, she realized a light was shining on her window, so she got up. When she got up, Selena saw that Francesca was sucking Alejandro's dick with a blindfold on. She quickly looked back and then got on her knees. She looked again, and what she saw was what caught her attention the most.

Selena saw Alejandro slapping Francesca in the face really hard; while she sucked his dick, he slapped her continuously. Selena watched this from the window, unable to move; she wanted to see everything she was seeing; Alejandro then turned around, making eye contact with Selena. Selena still did not move. Alejandro took his dick out of his wife's mouth; she still had her blindfold on. He then ejaculated on Francesca's face, then slapped her with his dick to get all the sperm out.

"Hold on, honey," he said.

While Francesca stood still on her knees with her mouth open and cum running all over her face, Alejandro walked to the window, held his dick, and started to stroke his dick with his right hand while he looked at Selena. Selena continuously looked at Alejandro stroking his dick and looking at her, full eye contact. She then caught herself and quickly ran from the window.

She then grabbed her bible and started praying.

"Dear lord, please forgive me; the temptation is very strong; I'm trying my very best," said Selena. She then put her bible under her pillow and grabbed her rosary.

She then went to bed.

NEXT MORNING

Mary had gone to town, leaving a note for Selena. She read the note, it said.

"Hey Sel, just went to get some shoes for you, be back in 3 hours, breakfast on the table."

Moments after eating breakfast, she was now relaxing by herself, pacing back and forth, thinking about the sex; nonstop, she thought about the slaps, the dick stroking, the blindfold. She then got up and started walking around. She went upstairs and put the same clothes back on that she had on yesterday. She went back downstairs. She then sat back down around the dinner table; she then saw a red light blinking on a certain device that was on the kitchen counter. She got up, she looked at the device, it was an answering machine, and there was a voice message waiting, but Selena didn't know what it was. To her, it was just another technology, and she totally ignored it.

Not able to control her wild thoughts anymore, she found a way that could make her visit the neighbor's house.

"This will work," she said to herself.

She hesitated not, and she went to the couple's house, Big, Bad, and Bold.

There she stood, hesitating to knock, having doubts about whether coming here was a good idea. She knocked, and Alejandro answered the door.

"Oh! Selena, how may I help you?" he asked.

Selena looked at him without saying a word. He looked at her.

"I WANT YOU TO DO ME LIKE YOU DID YOUR WIFE," Selena said abruptly.

"Who is it, honey?" Francesca asked.

"The neighbor, she is just returning the cakepan," he said. He then stepped outside and closed the door behind him.

"What are you talking about?" he asked her.

"What you did to your wife," Selena said. The man looked at Selena with a passionate look. He then squeezed his dick, walked over to Selena, and started to whisper in her ears.

He said, "Okay, come over later when my wife is gone." Alejandro then squeezed Selena's little ass very aggressively. "Nice jeans," he said. Selena smiled and went back to her house.

Moments later, and Francesca had left the house, Alejandro then signaled from his kitchen window, telling Selena to come over now. As she waited by her bedroom window, she hesitated not; she went straight over to Alejandro's house. Upon walking, Selena ran into the mailman as he was about to put the mail in the box.

"Good afternoon," she said to him as he put the mail in the mailbox and pinned something on the door. Selena paid no mind to it. She went straight on ahead.

"Someone is in a hurry," the mailman said to himself.

She got in, and Alejandro took her to the master bedroom, where you could still see Francesca's panties on the floor. Selena instantly went on her knees, with her mouth wide open; the husband instantly got stiff and started to rub Selena's face with his dick, still in his pants. As she used her teeth to bite his shorts, she started moaning.

"Where is the blindfold?" she asked.

"It's right here," he said. He then grabbed it and quickly put the blindfold on her, and she bit her lips.

"Virgin?" Alejandro asked.

"Yes," she said while she moaned, unable to see a thing.

"Aren't you a Christian?" he asked.

"Yes," she said while she moaned.

"Aren't Christians more self-reserved?" asked Alejandro.

"God will understand," said Selena. "Can you please put it in my mouth now?" she further asked.

Alejandro got turned on by Selena's slow talking; he whipped his dick out—8 inches long—and he started fucking Selena in the mouth, Selena now spitting all over Alejandro's dick as she choked and gagged. She then licked the uncircumcised tip and then pushed it down her throat. She started to choke again, and Alejandro moaned. Selena pulled the dick out of her mouth.

"Slap me in my face," she said. She then pushed the dick back into her mouth.

The guy started slapping her hard, and Selena's moaning got stronger; Alejandro grabbed her throat.

"Slap me," Selena said again. He slapped her again.

"Harder," she said.

Pow! Alejandro had given Selena a double hand slap on both cheeks at the same time. Selena started shaking rapidly. "Are you okay?" he asked, in a horny voice as he leaned his head back

"Ahhhhh!!" Alejandro screamed out in pain; he looked down, and blood was spraying all over; Selena's face and mouth were now full of blood,

"What the fuck was that?" he asked.

Selena had come down with an asthma attack from the double hand slap and had bit Alejandro's dick right off; that piece of his dick fell to the floor right on Francesca's panty. In a panic, he kicked her, and Selena went flying. Her asthma came on much stronger, and she started shaking. Alejandro was losing a lot of blood, and he then dropped to the floor and started shaking as well. Unfortunately, Selena died from the asthma attack, and Alejandro suffered major blood loss and died as well.

Mary now came home, and she parked at the front. She got out of the car with three shoe boxes in her hands. She then went to the mailbox and grabbed the mail. She then took the pinned paper from off the door, looked at it, and read it. After finishing reading it, she shouted, "Who the hell is Andre Paul?"

"You got one of those, too? I think he is a local writer, and he is giving away unreleased books to a lucky customer, who supports his talk show," said Francesca.

"You have never heard of Andre Paul?" Francesca asked.

"Nope, not until today," she said.

"Well, let me tell you about Andre Paul," said Francesca, when suddenly Mary heard the phone ringing inside her house.

"You can tell me another time, okay?" she said to Francesca and then went into the house. Francesca went inside her house as well.

She missed the call. She then saw the voice message still waiting, and she pressed play. It started playing, and the computer voice started talking—you know, that voice before the actual message begins. While waiting, she heard a very loud scream coming from the neighbor's house. "Was that Francesca," she said.

"Sel!" she shouted; no answer. She thought maybe she was just sleeping. She quickly grabbed her cardigan, and as she made her way to the neighbor's house, upon leaving, the message started playing. It said,

"HEY, SISTER, IT'S ME, DAVID. IRIS AND I ARE HEADING YOUR WAY. SELENA HAD FORGOTTEN HER INHALER PUMP, PLUS TELL HER WE GOT SOMETHING NEW FOR HER CALL, VICKS VAP-O-RUB. THIS WILL HELP WITH HER ASTHMA. SEE YOU SOON, SISTER."

[THE FIVE BUCKS]

Never ever thought I would live to see the day when five bucks were worth more than $5 million. It was

DECEMBER 1999, WINTER.

Millionaire Ted Campbell, the black owner of six local plazas all over Lennord County, was an extremely peaceful man who condemned the use of violence, even though he had learned how to shoot a gun at a tender age. The millionaire had two bodyguards that protected him, with loaded weapons, and went everywhere he went. He stood 5 feet 11 inches tall, had a low faded haircut, mostly wore a blue NePA University golf hat, had bulky muscles, and wore tightly fitted button shirts, mostly white, with tuxedo pants and expense shoes. He loved his colognes and kept a variety of them on his dresser. Ted enjoyed his time at work but spent most of it with his five-year-old daughter, Sky Campbell, who had brain cancer and was currently admitted to the Lennord County Hospital in King Town. Sky is 5 feet tall, a light-skinned black girl who took the color from her mom, who also had died of brain cancer. Sky is bald-headed; they had to shave her head due to the chemotherapy treatment, and she is mostly staying in the hospital; Ted visited Sky back and forth; the doctor said she has four more days to live, but unfortunately, Sky didn't know this information. What a sad situation, you might say, but what was even sadder was that Ted's birthday fell on the same day.

DAY ONE, DECEMBER 11TH

At 10 am, Ted had just woken up in his million-dollar home in NePa Town. Bodyguards were already outside, dressed and ready to take Mr. Campbell on his daily morning runs he takes every 9 am. One of the bodyguards had noticed Ted was taking longer than usual.

"Yo, I'm a check on the boss; he should've been out by now," said Carl,

The chief bodyguard, who was also responsible for the security of Ted's Plazas, a big 6-foot white guy, with huge muscles and looked like a wrestler, stretching out a tuxedo suit, with a bald head, carried an earpiece and two triangle mouth Desert Eagle guns.

"Sure, I will wait right here," said Edward, a 5-foot 9-inch Indian man with a bang hairstyle and with a neatly cut beard. He dressed like Carl, just with a thinner body, and wore an earpiece as well.

Carl went in, standing in the living room. "Boss," he shouted, but he heard nothing, "Boss, you not going for your morning run?" he asked, still nothing. He then went upstairs, and he heard crying in the master bedroom; he knocked on the door.

"Boss you, okay?" he asked. Still no answer, Carl barged into Ted's room and saw him masturbating to his wife's picture while crying nonstop.

"Oh shit!" said Carl, as he quickly stepped back out and closed the room door.

"Boss! I will wait for you outside," he said. Carl then headed back downstairs and quickly got back outside, laughing while walking towards Edward, who was leaning on a black Hummer.

"Yo Edward, I just caught the boss choking the rabbit," he said.

Edward started laughing, "Shit, we got to get the boss laid," he said.

"Yeah, but on a serious note, he is in a lot of pain; he was crying while doing it," said Carl.

"I see, with his wife and now his daughter, damn! I hate cancer," said Edward.

"Yes, after today, three more days," said Carl.

"I know, truly makes me sad; I raised that little girl," said Edward.

"I know, and that is why we have to be strong for the boss," said Carl.

"I know. Ted is a very upfront and decent guy; he deserves the best," said Edward.

Moments later, Ted is now coming out, in his champion sweat suit, with gloves and hoody,

"Ready, boss," said Carl. "Yes, while he wipes his eyes.

They all got in the black Hummer, Carl driving, Edward in the passenger seat; Ted likes to sit in the back.

They drove off, merged on 9W, heading to the walkway bridge in Poughkeepsie, NY. There they are cruising, Ted looking through the window, not doing much talking, thinking about Sky. The visit was at 5 in the afternoon.

"Boss, I want you to know I don't judge you," said Carl as he looked through the rare view mirror at Ted.

"I know that, Carl," said Ted.

"Hey, boss, I want you to know, I'm truly sorry for Sky. You know she is like a daughter to me," said Edward.

"Thank you, Edward, and I know that," said Ted.

Moments later.

They came up to the walkway bridge. They pulled over to the entrance of the bridge. Ted got out and put his hoody on.

"Boss, we will meet you at the end," said Carl and drove off.

Ted started jogging on the walkway, which was a mile long; upon running, Ted started crying again, tears flowing down his cheeks. A vision of Sky, in the hospital bed, with all her hair shaved off, stays dormant in his mind. He then stopped suddenly; while resting, he saw two old white women sitting on the bench below the big American flag, talking about some robbery that had taken place the night before,

"I heard two of them are women and from Poughkeepsie," one of the old ladies said.

Ted paid no mind to it and started running, again, half a mile to go; he started running faster. Moments after reaching the other side of the bridge, his bodyguards were already waiting for him. Ted walked up to them; he got in, they gave him a Gatorade, and they drove off. Upon driving, Carl asked Ted how the run was, and he told him, it was one mile, they all laughed, and it was like that the entire ride home.

Moments later, Ted got home, took a shower, and then went to visit his daughter. The visit was a great visit.

DAY 2, DECEMBER 12TH

11 am, Ted was still in bed, eyes wide open, in deep thought, when he suddenly grabbed his wife's photo and started to masturbate, stroking his dick under the sheet while he held firm to his wife's picture. Ted then ejaculated on the picture frame.

Several minutes later, after cleaning up himself, he was now getting ready for his morning run; Nike sweat suit on, he got out and saw only Edward,

"Good morning, Eddy," said Ted. "Good morning, boss," Edward replied.

"Where is Carl?" he asked.

"Boss, you must be really tired, man," said Edward. "And what do you mean by that?" Ted asked him.

"Boss, remember Carl was telling us that he heard that a couple of thieves are in Lennord County and fishing around the plaza," said

Edward. "I think he said they are from Poughkeepsie," Edward further said.

"Oh yes, and yes, I'm tired; I'm not sleeping properly," Ted replied.

"Boss, I know you love your wife, but it's been four years now; you don't think it's time you start dating again?" Edward asked.

"Great suggestion Edward, just bad timing," Ted replied.

"Oh, I'm sorry," he replied. "I wasn't trying to disrespect Sky or anything like that. I was just looking out for you," Edward further said.

"I know that, Edward. You have been working for me for seven years now; I know who you are inside," Ted replied.

Moments later, Ted and Edward drove off, and they got to the walkway in 20 minutes. The result was the same as yesterday; Ted was extremely sad, and while he jogged, he thought about Sky. Then he met his bodyguard on the other side of the bridge. *Such an awful situation to be in; not even his money can cheer him up.*

Edward was already waiting at the bride, vehicle running, heat maxed, car cozy warmed. Ted jumped in, Edward gave him a Gatorade, then took him home; after that, he went to see his daughter; the visit was a great visit.

DAY 3, DECEMBER 13TH
12 P.M. IN THE AFTERNOON

Ted is still in bed, eyes wide open, thinking nonstop. He started crying. He looked at his wife's photo, stared at it for minutes, then grabbed it, stared at it intensely, then started to masturbate, holding firm to his wife's photo, he then stopped suddenly, put the picture frame down, looked at himself in the dresser mirror, with his dick in his hand, he spoke,

"This is not working," he said. And suddenly remembered what Edward had said to him about moving on. He then grabbed a towel and went straight to the bathroom. He then took a shower and then headed outside. He was now walking toward the Hummer and realized Carl wasn't there.

"Carl is at the plaza again?" he asked Edward.

"Yes, said he wants to make sure he misses nothing," said Edward.

"Yeah, I trust Carl with my life," said Ted.

Moments later, they got to the Poughkeepsie Walkway bridge. Using the same procedure, Edward went to the other side of the bridge and

Ted started running, but after about 3/4 of a mile in, Ted had come stop. He was taking a rest when he saw a big-assed light-skinned black woman with long braided hair, resembling his wife in body, but her face was completely different. He looked at her, and she looked at him. She then bent over, showing her ass in her tight black leggings; it caught Ted's attention, and he couldn't take his eye off it. She got back up and ran off, and he started chasing her. He pulled up beside her,

"You are beautiful," he said while they were still jogging. "Thank you, you not bad yourself," she replied.

"Can I take you out?" he asked.

"That was fast," she replied.

They both came to a full stop and started looking at each other, "You got a phone?' she asked. "Yes," he said. He then took his phone out and took her number.

"Don't waste it," she said and ran off, leaving Ted staring at her butt.

"What is your name?" he asked.

"Natalie," she replied.

Moments later, Ted was now making his way back to the car, smiling and blushing. He pulled to the Hummer; Edward was already outside on the bonnet, and he saw Ted smiling from a distance.

"Boss, what happened? I have not seen you smile like this since the passing of Kiesha," he said as he smiled, too. Ted didn't indulge in the conversation. He jumped in, and Edward got off the hood, got in as well, handed Ted a Gatorade, then sped off.

They got home, and Ted told Edward to take the night off; he then got out of the Hummer and walked to the step of the house. Edward, now driving off with the Hummer, stopped at Ted's foot, winded the window down, and spoke.

"Boss, tell Sky I say hi," said Edward.

"Sure, Eddy," he said.

"Which car are you driving?" Edward asked.

"The Maserati," Ted said.

"My guy," said Edward.

He then sped off.

Unfortunately, that evening, Ted had chosen to make a dinner reservation with the new girl, Natalie, instead of seeing Sky. It was a no-show.

DAY 4, DECEMBER 14TH

The predicted day of Sky Campbell's death has come. It was now 1 pm in the afternoon; Ted was still in bed with the woman he brought out for dinner, both wrapped up naked under the sheets. Ted had turned his wife's picture frame downwards; the woman then rolled over on him and started to rub his chest.

"Happy birthday, darling," she said.

"Thank you," he said, "You don't think we are moving too fast?" he further asked her.

"If you are looking for a wife, then yes!" she replied and started to feel Ted's balls.

They kissed, and he started to feel her up. He was now fingering her, and she was moaning. He wasted no time; he got between her legs and began ramming her; then a sudden knock came from outside the room door,

"I will be out in a second, Edward," he said. He then ground slowly between Natalie's legs. Natalie made a low moan sound as she ground her teeth.

"Sir, it's Carl. It's 1:10 now; aren't you going for your run?" he asked.

She moaned; Carl heard the moaning, and Ted then stopped.

"Not running today, Carl, but can you please give me 30 minutes? I will be right out," said Ted.

"Okay, and happy birthday sir," Carl said. "Thank you' he replied.

Carl was now making his way out, walking fast to tell Edward what he had heard. Edward saw him coming, "Why are you smiling like that?" Edward asked.

"The boss is pounding some bimbo in his room," said Carl. "Yeah, he met her last night," said Edward.

"You don't think it was too quick to bring her here?" Carl asked.

"Plus, today is, you know what," Carl further said.

"True, but the boss is overdue for some flesh, so I don't think he is going to wait," said Edward.

"Must be a skank in that bed," Carl replied. They both laughed.

Moments later, and it was now 2 p.m., Ted and Natalie were now making their way out. Ted was dressed in a white button down, tucked in his blue tuxedo pants, and no belt with white Air Force 1, and Natalie was wearing a tight leather suit while she held Ted's trench coat. Both walked down towards the Hummer, where Edward and Carl were. Ted then introduced Natalie.

"This is Natalie. I met her in Poughkeepsie," he said. "Hi Natalie, I'm Carl, and this is Edward," said Carl. "Hello," she replied, "You are very beautiful," Carl said.

"Thank you," she replied as she flashed her long braided hair. "You were just calling her a bimbo, you asshole," said Edward under his breath; no one could hear him.

"Boss, you don't think you should be at the hospital earlier today?" Carl asked Ted.

"It is okay; I will go at 5," he replied. "But boss, she is," Carl replied. "Carl, stop! Please!" said Ted. "Okay," Carl replied.

"A matter of fact, let us all go out for lunch," said Ted

"Where?" Natalie asked.

"P&G," said Ted.

"Where is that?" she asked.

"91 Main Street, Nepa Town," Ted replied.

"Ready when you're ready, boss," said Edward.

Moments later, they all went to lunch and back; it was now 3:30 in the afternoon. Ted and Natalie went back to the house. Carl and Edward stood outside in the Hummer Truck.

AN HOUR AND 15 MINUTES LATER.

At 4:45 in the afternoon, Carl and Edward had just woken up from a nap they both took in the Hummer, realized the time, and quickly rushed to wake Ted to remind him about his daughter when he got in. He saw Ted fast asleep on the couch, in his robe untied, with his dick out, with a big champagne bottle in his hand, and Natalie was searching around the house. He stepped to her.

"What are you looking for?" Carl asked her.

"Nothing, I was just giving Ted some head, and he fell asleep, so I decided to look around for a little bit," she said while she tightened her robe.

Carl then tossed a blanket over Ted, then woke him up, "Sir, you don't want to be late for Sky," he said.

"Shit, what time is it?" he asked.

"Sir, it's 4:49," he said.

"Shit, let me get dressed." He jumped up; the blanket fell off, and his dick was exposed. He quickly gathered himself and walked off to the bedroom.

Moments later, a taxi came for Natalie; Ted and his bodyguards were already on their way to King Town.

Cruising on 9W. "Sir, did you enjoy yourself?" Edward asked.

Ted smiled and said, "She is a freak; my wife would've never sucked my dick."

"That is a good wife," said Carl.

Ted immediately got silent and reverted to a sad face. Edward and Carl both saw that.

"Why don't you tell us about Sky Campbell," said Edward as he tried to change the topic.

Ted then looks through the car window, gazing at the wooded areas of Lennord County as they cruise.

"Better yet, let me tell you a story about Sky," he replied as he smiled.

Ted had told a very beautiful story about him and Sky; the story was touching, and it made Edward cry.

Moments later, Ted arrived at the hospital, pulled up at the front, and got out of the car.

"We will wait out here," said Carl.

"Okay," Ted replied and quickly closed the door.

He started to walk, crying his eyes out as he entered the hospital. Up the stairs he went, passing the big glass windows. He was now on the second floor, only 40 feet away from Sky's room. He then saw a man dressed in all white, like a doctor, coming out of Sky's room, with nurses shaking his hand; the man quickly walked away. Ted got to the room door and greeted the nurses. Sky was asleep.

"Who was that man?" he asked.

"That was Andre Paul. Sky had requested to see him after seeing him on TV last night," said the nurse. "Where were you? She asked for you nonstop," she further said.

"I was caught up with work, but what do you mean by 'requested to see him'? Who is this Andre Paul?" Ted asked.

"Andre Paul is a local writer who has a talk show on channel 12; Sky had asked to meet him, so the Director of the hospital arranged it," she said.

"But what is strange is that he actually showed up," said the nurse while she smiled.

"Okay, is he famous or something?" he asked.

"Not really, he is a local book writer, a very handsome and charming man; he doesn't care about money," said the nurse. "Plus, he is," she further said.

"He is what?" Ted asked.

Sky then suddenly made a loud cough. Ted quickly ran to her; she was awake.

"Baby, I'm here. Everything will be okay," he said.

"Dad is that you?" she asked as she coughed.

"Yes, baby, and I will never leave you," he said.

"Where were you last night?" Sky asked.

"Daddy was at Mommy's grave," he said. Sky coughed some more, and her dad hugged her and placed his palm on her bald head. He started crying,

"Happy birthday, Daddy," said Sky. As she went under her pillow to grab something, she pulled out $5 dollars; she handed it to him.

"This is all I have, Dad," she said while she coughed.

"Thank you, baby," he said as he accepted the five dollars.

"The doctor said I will get better soon," said Sky.

"Yes," said Ted while he looked at the nurses.

Then suddenly, Sky's life machine started to flatline. She was now shaking. Her dad grabbed her; the cancer had rapidly spread all over her brain, spreading like wildfire.

"Doctor," said Ted, as he looked at Sky foaming with a seizure, shaking in his arms.

"Doctor, please help!" said Ted, eyes filled with tears. The doctor was unable to do anything, and after two minutes of vigorous shaking, Sky stopped responding.

Sky Campbell was pronounced dead right in her dad's arms, leaving Ted the most distraught human being on planet Earth. The doctors were now chasing Ted out of the room as they attended to Sky's dead body. Ted went back outside, where Carl and Edward were waiting for him; they saw his face and knew it was that time.

"My condolences," said Edward, and out of nowhere, Ted replied with a "Shit happens," he quickly got in the car.

"Just take me home," he further said. Carl looked at Edward in total silence. They drove off.

Moments later, distraught and confused, Ted was now making his way home with nothing but the five bucks in his pocket and his two bodyguards.

He got home, and the bodyguards remained outside. Ted then went to his room, put the five dollars on his dresser next to his wife's picture, and went to lie down. Moments later, he was twisting and turning, feeling sadness and confusion all at once. Ted started thinking of ways to ease his pain.

"Should I call this freak?" he asked himself. He then tried calling Natalie, but he got no answer. It went straight to voicemail.

"Fuck it," he said. Then went to bed.

4 HOURS LATER.

While resting, Ted heard a noise coming from downstairs.

"Carl? Is that you, Eddy?" he asked. No answer. "Carl," he said again.

Still no answer—he then got up, and as he was about to open the door, five gunmen dressed in all black with black ski masks burst in, pointing high-powered rifles at Ted.

"Get on the fucking ground, and don't move," one gunman said.

"Carl!" Ted shouted.

"You mean the dead bodyguards outside?" he asked Ted sarcastically.

"Don't give me any reason to kill you; we are only here to rob you," the robber said while the other four stood in the back.

"Where is the money?" he asked.

"Everything is in that safe; the pin is 3535. Take everything; I don't care," said Ted.

All five robbers looked at each other. The lead robber then went to the safe and tried to open it; it was indeed 3535. "She was right," the robber said to himself. They later opened the safe and took everything out; over five million dollars was confiscated. One by one, they loaded up the bags.

"This one is kind; we won't kill him," said the lead robber.

"But boss, we don't take prisoners, remember," said another robber, who was holding two duffle bags of cash.

"Not this time," said the leader. "Let's go," he further said.

On their way out, the lead robber grabbed the five-dollar bill that was on the dresser next to his wife's picture.

"Please, take everything except that five dollars," said Ted. The thief ignored him.

"Everything is coming with us, negro," he said.

Ted tried to tackle the thief—POW! A shot went off. Ted dropped to the ground, and the thieves took off. They got in their car and drove away.

Moments later, Ted was now getting up; it was just a flesh wound. He screamed out in anger, then quickly walked to the bathroom, quickly patched himself up. With rage pouring out of him, all he is thinking about is the five bucks his daughter gave him. He then got outside and saw Carl and Edward both dead in the Hummer. He quickly grabbed Carl's guns and touched his forehead.

"Rest in peace, Carl," he said.

Quickly, he got in his black Ferrari and drove off. Ted was now tracking the money, with a tracker that had been placed on each bill, just in case something like this should ever happen, and with two chrome Desert Eagle handguns and a mind full of vengeance. Ted sped through Lennord County, following the thieves, when suddenly the robbers came to a full stop.

Ted found his way to the location: it was an abandoned house behind Nepa University. The car was empty; they had already gotten inside. Ted quickly parked down the street, grabbed his jacket, grabbed the guns, and walked to the building. He heard talking, but he hesitated not; he busted in, pointing his Desert Eagles at all five robbers.

"NOBODY FUCKING MOVE," said Ted as he pulsated in anger.

The thieves were frightened. Ted was now looking at them, defenseless. They had all left their guns in the car; the money was thrown out on a table.

"NATALIE," said Ted, as he stared at her in deep rage. "What are you doing here?" Ted asked Natalie as he got a quick vision of her riding his cock.

"I said, what the fuck are you doing here? Are you a part of this shit?" he further asked. She still did not answer.

"Make sense, why I wasn't getting our phone, you little bitch," said Ted.

"Why?" he asked.

"Isn't it obvious she tricked you, you fool?" said the leader, a skinny white man with an army-style haircut.

"She only fucked you so we could get info on your house," he further said while he laughed.

"Is this true, Natalie?" Ted asked. She still had not answered.

Ted then took a quick glance and saw the five-dollar bill in Natalie's hand, and at that point, he didn't care anymore. He gave it no thought; Ted instantly shot Natalie in the head, and the others quickly scattered. Ted squeezed off a few more rounds—another woman got shot in her head, marrow splashed all over the millions, and all three guys got shot in the chest. Ted walked over to the leader and pointed his gun at him.

"Please, don't kill me," he begged.

Ted tossed both guns to the side, kneeled, and started to punch the shit out of the leader's face, punching nonstop. He then stopped, got back up, and started screaming. He then walked over to Natalie, looking at her with a bullet hole in her face, and grabbed the five bucks. He looked at the $5 million on the table and walked away. He then made his way to his car, heading back to his house.

Moments after getting back, he pulled into the driveway and then parked. He heard coughing coming from the Hummer; it was Edward— he was still alive,

"Eddy," said Ted.

"Boss, is that you?" said Edward,

Ted quickly rushed to Edward and pulled him out of the truck. He was coughing up blood; he then grabbed Ted's jacket and pulled him closer.

"It was him all along," said Edward.

While he pointed to the passenger seat at what seemed to be a bulletproof vest with a bullet already lodged in it, Edward then coughed, looking like he was not going live any longer. Then he spoke.

"I DON'T HAVE LONG, SO LISTEN CAREFULLY. WHAT I AM ABOUT TO TELL YOU WILL COME AS A SHOCK TO YOU,

BUT IT WAS CARL ALL ALONG. CARL WAS THE ONE WHO PLANNED THE WHOLE THING. HE WAS WORKING WITH THE PEOPLE WHO ROBBED YOU—EVEN THAT BITCH NATALIE, SHE IS CARL'S FUCK TOY. PLEASE, DON'T LET HIM GET AWAY WITH THIS. KILL THEM ALL; DO IT FOR SKY, AND ONE LAST THING, HAPPY BIRTHDAY, BOSS."

[THE TROOPER REAPER]

Tony and Tyler Whittaker both live in Midtown with their mother; Tony suffers from mental illness, unable to make something of his life, while Tyler, on the other hand, is currently in junior college (SUNY ORANGE), where he is pursuing a finance degree. You could say he is well on his way to a great future, for he hopes to be the first black president.

Tony is constantly on anti-depressant medication, which helps him to calm down. He stands 6 feet 1 inch tall, is 23 years old, with dark skin and low-cut hair, weighs about 195 pounds, and is always wearing baggy blue jean pants with baggy flannels. Tony can often be seen talking to himself, it is a symptom of his illness, and also, he spends most of his time in the basement, mainly because of the quiet toilet time he gets; he says he finds peace there.

Tyler is a skinny young man with dark skin and a mohawk hairstyle, 20 years old, weighing about 140 pounds, 5 feet 9 inches tall, dressed mostly in skinny black jeans, black boots, and a black European-style trench coat.

The siblings are very close; they do get along but do bump heads sometimes due to Tony's condition, and he often reminds Tony of them.

Like this one time, when Tony was pretending to have a million dollars and went to Tyler, telling him to hold on to it, he would be back later for it.

This is how it all went down. Tyler was on the back porch doing homework. Tony walked up to Tyler and said.

"Hey bro, here is a million," said Tony. Then he opened his palm, and there was nothing in it. He continued to speak, "Hey, Tyler, keep this million for me," he said.

"But you gave me nothing," Tyler replied.

"Just be cool, man, and keep that for me; I might borrow some later," said Tony.

He then walked off and headed down Academy Ave.

Moments later, Tony was now coming back to Tyler; smiling from a distance, he approached him.

"Yo! Tyler, let me get $50 out of that million I gave you earlier," he said to Tyler.

Tyler laughed and said, "Can you chill with that." Tony looked at him and laughed.

Here is the strangest thing about the whole situation, Tyler thinks it's a joke, but Tony is dead ass serious, serious as a judge.

"Bro, run the $50," said Tony to Tyler.

"I said, cut it out, man," said Tyler.

But what got Tyler upset was Tony kept grabbing the pocket of his pants and pulling on it.

"What is wrong with you, man?" he asked Tony, Tony, still pulling on Tyler's pocket.

"Here you go, man," he said. He handed him the $50. at the time, Tyler had just gotten paid, for he was working at the college as a student worker for the finance department.

Tyler always has understanding for Tony's feelings and sympathizes with his older brother. He was always looking out for him and trying his best to keep him out of trouble. Tony liked to walk the streets too often. So, things between them remain moderately mutual.

It was the year 1989. It was a Monday morning: November 13th, cold as hell.

Tyler was getting ready for school, which was just a five-minute walk from the house. Plus, his first class started in the next 45 minutes.

Tyler lives on Houston Ave, Midtown, and his school is at 115 South Street, Midtown.

He went to the kitchen to get breakfast; his mom had made banana fritters with saltfish and cabbage.

"Good morning, Mommy," he said.

"Good morning, Tyler," replied the mother of Tyler.

Sandra Cook. Standing 5 feet 8 inches tall, a light-skinned black woman who fluctuates between wigs, natural hair down to her shoulder, black eyes, blue contact lenses, attractive body, dressed very stylish but mostly wore sweatpants and baggy shirts when she was home.

"I already shared yours; it's in the microwave," Sandra further said as she sat at the table, stringing a needle that she held in her hand.

"Thank you," Tyler replied.
"Your welcome, son," said Sandra.

Tyler then grabbed his plate and sat around the dinner table in the kitchen; Sandra then poked the stringed needle into the wall, with the thread hanging down. She then got up and attended to the dishes.

"Where is Tony?" he asked.
"He is in the basement," said Sandra. "Oh," he replied.

Moments later, after finishing eating, he decided to take a shower. The bathroom was next to the kitchen; he got in, and turned the water on, letting it warm up, then went to grab his towel. Upon passing his mom, she shouted.

"If you know you are going to take a shit first, don't turn the water on now," she said.

Tyler laughed and continued walking.

"I'm serious; I need to take a shower, too. I'm leaving for work soon," she said.

Sandra is a registered nurse who works at the Lennord County Hospital in King Town.

"Okay, Mom," he replied, then headed for his room.

He then grabbed his towel and headed straight for the bathroom. Moments later, you could hear Tyler shitting and loud shit noise came from the toilet.

"Boy! I know your ass wanted to shit," said Sandra to Tyler. Tyler laughed while he forced the shit out.

"Why don't you use the toilet in the basement?" Sandra asked.

"Because I don't like it when I'm down there, and Tony comes knocking on the door, saying this is his domain," said Tyler while he chuckled.

"Well, you tell Tony when he starts paying bills in this house, he can have that toilet as his throne," said Sandra while she chuckled. Tyler laughed as well.

Moments later, Tyler had finished bathing, and was now getting dressed, having already moisturized his body with cocoa butter lotion, greased his mohawk with Dax hair oil and was now fighting to get in his skinny jeans. He then put on a skinny long-sleeved black shirt and tucked it in his pants; no belt was added. He then put on his black high topped winter boots, sat on the bed, and laced them. Then, Tony walked in, coming in through the front door, a green door. Tony looked at Tyler sitting on the bed; he quickly walked over, smiling from a distance.

"Brother, can you give me a joke?" Tony asked Tyler. Tyler looked at him, and then he sighed.

"I don't have time for a joke right now," said Tyler. By now, Sandra was already in the shower, steaming her face off in the warm water.

"No problem, you can give it to me when you get back home from school," said Tony. He then walked away, heading for the kitchen. Tony was now looking around, talking to himself while he looked for his breakfast.

"What happens if Jesus doesn't come back? That means I will be the one taking over," he said to himself as he made his way to the bathroom.

"Knock! Knock!

"Yes!" Sandra shouted.

"Hey, Mommy, is that my food on the table?" he asked.

"Yes," she replied.

"Okay, thanks, Mom," he said.

"What?" she asked.

"I said 'thanks,'," Tony replied.

"Oh, you're welcome, Tony," she replied.

Tony grabbed his food and then sat down and started to eat. Tyler was now making his way out, ready to go to school. He opened the front door. The big green door; he turned around.

"Tony, tell Mom I left," he said.

"Okay, brother, and remember the joke later," he replied.

"Sure," Tyler replied.

Moments later, Tyler was now making his way to school, the route he takes is literally a five-minute walk, and it was just one straight road, all Eastmain Ave, that merged into South Street. He was now walking, moving very fast, with his hands in his trench coat pockets, a black school bag with a Guinness logo on it.

He arrived and quickly rushed to Algebra class.

SUNY ORANGE was a compound consisting of four big white buildings, north, south, east, and west, with a big green and white gate. His class was to the north. Tyler was now making his way to the classroom. He got in and sat down, and the professor was erasing something off the board while all the students took their seats. Tyler took his algebra textbook out with a composition notebook, then put his bag under his seat. The professor spoke.

"Did you all know today is a pop quiz?" she said. Professor Corbridge, a tall, skinny grey haired white woman with glasses dressed like a Librarian.

"If it is a pop quiz, then why did you tell us?" asked Tyler. The class laughed.

"Are you ready for the quiz, Mr. Whittaker?" Mrs. Corbridge asked Tyler as she looked under her glasses.

"Yes, ma'am," he replied.

"Okay, there will be five questions, do only three of them, please, any three you like," she said.

She was now handing out the pop quiz; one by one, she handed each student a paper; there were about 25 students. Moments later, everyone was now with a paper; Tyler was now looking at the questions. "Damn, I should've studied," he said to himself. He read the questions.

Questions
1. $3x + 2y - 5$
2. $2x + 4y - 7$
3. $4x - 10 + 10y$
4. $2x^2 - 3xy + 5$
5. $4y - 7x - 6y - 8$

"Begin now," said Mrs. Corbridge, while she walked around with her creepy self, always wearing a long skirt and cardigans. Moments later, she went back to her desk.

Tyler took questions 1, 2, and 5. It took him 20 minutes, and he hesitated to hand it in, thinking he had finished too fast. He did hand it in, walked up to the teacher's desk, and gave the paper to the professor.

"Finished already, Mr. Whittaker?" said the professor staring intently at the worksheet under her glasses.

"Yes, ma'am," he replied.

"Okay, and what does this say?" she asked.

"What does, what say?" Tyler asked.

"This here at the bottom of your test," She then pointed to the bottom of the paper. "Read it," she said. Tyler started reading it.

"'See the back of page for question 6,' Oh!" he further said, then flipped it around. He then read question 6, which said: "Do you want a chance to win an unreleased book from Andre Paul?"

"Do you know who Andre Paul is?" the professor asked.

"Yes, I do; he sponsors our library," he said.

"Who is Andre Paul?" asked the second student to finish the quiz.

"Tyler, why don't you tell Mr. Williams, who Andre Paul is," said the professor.

"SSHHHHHHSSHH!" said the closest student to the conversation. "Some of us are still working," she said as she continued with her quiz.

"Mr. Whittaker, you and Mr. Williams can both leave," said the professor. "Just remember, end of term test is next week," she further said.

"Thank you, ma'am," said Tyler and Edward Williams, and they both left.

Tyler was now making his way home, walking at a moderate pace down Eastmain Street, strolling as he usually does. Grabbing his CD player and headphones, he started to listen to music; it was "Under Me Sleng Teng," by Wayne Smith.

He started to sing along to the lyrics.

"Under me sleng teng, me under sleng teng, under me sleng teng, me under it, Heh! Heh! Way in my brain, no cocaine, I don't wanna, I don't wanna go insane, way in my brain, no cocaine, I don't wanna, I don't wanna go insane."

He was now getting closer to his house.

Pow! Pow! Pow! Pow! Pow! Pow! Six gunshots went off. He pulled one side of his headset off and looked around.

Pow! Pow! Pow! Pow! Pow! Another five gunshots went off; that was now 11 gunshots he heard. He took the headphone off completely and stopped the music. A Mexican guy was passing by who also heard the shots and was startled as well.

"Did just hear that?" he asked the guy.

"Yes, it sounded like it came from Sam's Chicken shop."

Tyler then felt a sudden pain in the center of his chest. He grabbed his chest; he paid no mind to it, and he continued walking.

Moments after getting home, he saw that his mom was still in the house. He walked in, and he greeted her with a "Hey, Mommy."

"I thought you had work?" he further asked.

"After I got out of the shower, I felt a sudden, strange feeling in my chest, and my migraine started acting up," she replied.

"Take some Tylenol," he said, "Where is Tony?" Tyler further asked.

"He went to follow this girl down by Sam's Chicken Shop. Do me a favor; when you get a chance, look and see if the kitchen knife has fallen behind the fridge. One is missing from the knife holder," said Sandra.

"Okay," said Tyler. "By the way, did you not hear those gunshots? They sounded like they were coming from Sam's Chicken Shop," he said.

"No, I didn't, but I am going to take a nap. My head hurts badly," said Sandra. She then went to her room, closed her door, and went straight to sleep.

Moments later, it was now nighttime, and Tony had not come home yet. It was unlike him to stay out late due to the fact he must take his medications. Tyler was now sitting on the couch in the living room that faced the green door as he was doing homework and listening to music. Then there was a sudden knock on the door.

Knock! Knock! Knock! It startled Sandra. Knock! Knock! Knock! On the door again.

"Tyler, who is that?" Sandra asked, still in her room. There was no answer from Tyler.

"Tyler, get the door," she said. Still no answer.

Knock! Knock! on the door again. Sandra got mad and came out to answer the door herself, dressed in grey sweatpants and a white baggy shirt with no bra.

"Those flipping headphones," she said as she looked at Tyler.

Sandra opened the door and saw two white men in long brown khaki trench coats standing upright, with brown felt hats, button-down shirts, and neckties, looking like government officials. It was two Midtown detectives.

"How may I help you gentlemen tonight?" Sandra asked.

"Ma'am, are you Sandra Cook?" they asked.

"Yes, I am," she replied.

"Is your son Tony Whittaker?" he asked.

Sandra's knees started shaking.

"Is this your son's jacket?" the other detective asked as he gave her a plastic bag with a bloody jacket in it. Sandra then looked at the jacket and realized it was Tony's.

"Yes, what happened?" she asked.

"Ma'am, I'm sorry to inform you, but your son, Tony, was shot and killed at Sam's Chicken Shop this afternoon by three Midtown police officers," the detective said.

Tyler couldn't hear anything; all he saw was his mother falling backward. She had fallen, she didn't pass out, but she was weak. Tyler quickly attended to her, lifted her up, and put her on the couch.

"Oh no, not Tony. Why, my lord? Why would you do this?" she said as she cried very loudly in pain.

"Mom, what is going on?" Tyler asked while he looked at the bloody jacket.

"They killed Tony," said Sandra; she then cried louder.

Then suddenly, Tyler paused in silence for about four seconds. He then let his mom go, looked at the detectives, then went to his room.

"Ma'am, we need you to come with us to identify the body," said one of the detectives. Sandra was crying—nonstop crying. The detective then went to take her up from the floor.

She then quickly put her robe on.

"Tyler, I will be right back," she said. Tyler didn't answer.

"He is probably sad at the moment," said one of the detectives.

Moments later, Sandra and the two detectives made their way to the morgue.

Unfortunately, it was Tony who got shot 11 times. They said he got into an altercation with a man in Sam's Chicken Shop. The owner said Tony was acting like a crazy person, chasing a man around the store with a sharp kitchen knife, and that was when the owner called the cops. The cops came to the scene when Tony was making his way out. He had a knife in his hand, and they told him to drop the knife, but he refused. Then Tony took a step towards the direction of his house, and that was when the cops shot him 11 times in the chest area, killing Tony on the spot.

Then Sandra had to go and give a statement at the police station. Tyler was still at the house.

Sobbing nonstop for his big brother Tony, he went on a rampage destroying everything in his room. The 20-year-old then rushed outside, took his mom's car, and sped off.

He was speeding on the lonely backroads of 9W, not watching his speed when suddenly a woman state trooper pulled him over for going too fast. Tyler pulled over, no other vehicle in sight; he was now crying his eyes out.

She got out of the car, a thick-assed white woman, with a tiny waist, with long blonde hair. She fixed her utility belt, then approached Tyler and didn't even ask him why he was crying.

"License and registration, please," she said as she shined the flashlight in Tyler's face.

"Officer, why did you pull me over?" he asked as he looked up at the flashlight.

"Sir, please give me your license!" she said.

"Or what?" said Tyler.

"Sir, don't let me ask again," said the officer. Tyler was looking up at her name badge. It said, "Officer Zimmerman."

"You want to kill me like you killed my fucking brother, bitch," said Tyler with a serious look on his face. The officer quickly got irritated.

"Sir, I already asked you twice," she said. "Sir, please get out of the car," she said. Tyler ignored her, then abruptly opened the door, knocking the trooper to the ground.

"I'm sorry," said Tyler while he stared at the officer wallowing in the dirt.

She immediately got back up and slapped Tyler on the head with her flashlight. She quickly pulled out her gun and pointed it at him. "Don't fucking move," she said.

"You going to shoot me?" Tyler asked, "Then go ahead, bitch!" he further said.

"Just give me a reason, you little punk," said Officer Zimmerman. She then grabbed him, turned him around, then pushed him hard into the car.

The trooper then handcuffed Tyler but with his hands in front of him. She looked at him. She slapped him on the head again, and his head started to bleed.

"Fucking idiot, I could've broken my leg," said Officer Zimmerman. While she pushed him back into the car, she then turned her back to Tyler, brushing the dirt off her uniform.

Then a sudden feeling of vengeance came over Tyler. After losing his brother earlier today by cops, and now getting abused by one, Tyler put his arms around the trooper's neck, pulled real hard, with the handcuff still on his wrist, dragging the officer backward. She fell on him. With all his might, he squeezed her throat. She tried hard to get from his grip. She tried to reach for her gun. Tyler kicked her in the back of her knees, and she fell to the ground on her knees. He then slammed her head to the ground. Tyler then lay beside the officer and continued to squeeze her throat, the trooper started foaming, but Tyler still held on to her. Moments later, the officer was unresponsive. Officer Zimmerman died in Tyler's arms. Several minutes later, Tyler was now coming to his senses, and he was now panicking.

"Ohmigod, what did I just do?" he asked himself as he looked left and right in a fast motion.

The officer had pissed on herself, leaking all over Tyler's pants. The pee instantly got cold on Tyler's skin; he was disgusted and pushed her off. Tyler now concluded that the officer was indeed dead. He checked her pulse one more time to make sure.

"Oh, my fucking god, this bitch is really dead," he said. He then looked at the piss mark between her legs, soaking her entire uniform.

He started to panic some more. He took the key from the officer's belt, opened the handcuffs, then put her body in his car. Leaving the cop car on site, he drove off, heading back to his house on Houston Ave. He was now driving on 9W, waiting for the Midtown exit to come up. He turned the radio on, he then turned it back off, he wound the window down, he wound it back up, he turned the heat on, and he turned it off.

"Am I going crazy like Tony?" he asked himself while he blew short of breath.

"Calm down, Tyler; she hit you first," he said. "She attacked you first," he said again.

"Should I report this? No, I can't. I will go to jail," he said. "I don't want to go to jail, ohmigod!" he further said.

"Think, Tyler, think," he said moments later. Tyler then looked at the officer's body in the back seat.

Tyler took Officer Zimmerman's body back to his house. Sandra was still at the police station. He took the officer's body to the basement and placed it on the ground. He was now walking around, pacing, and pondering. He grabbed the axe saw blade from the tool kit and started to saw the officer's hand off; he then realized her uniform was slowing down the cutting.

"I don't want to do this, but I have to," he said to himself. He did not hesitate.

Tyler took the officer's uniform off, leaving her cold dead body completely naked; he started to saw the arm again, the sound of the bone and saw was unwelcome for Tyler, but he kept on sawing. He got through the first arm and tossed it to the side. He sawed the next arm off. Now, both arms and legs were detached from the officer's body. He looked down at her torso looked at her vagina. Tyler stuck the saw in the officer's pussy and sawed all the way to her belly; he sawed her in two.

Twenty-five minutes later, Tyler had cut Zimmerman into tiny pieces; one by one, he flushed the pieces of flesh and bones down Tony's favorite toilet; the place was now full of blood. Tyler then went back outside and grabbed the bottle of bleach his mom kept in her car. He opened the trunk of the car, grabbed the bleach, and quickly went back inside and down the basement; he started to clean up, with tears flowing through his eyes.

"Brother, I have the joke now; please, wherever you are, please listen to me," he said. "Listen, the cow jumped over the moon," he further said, with tears running down his cheeks.

He started laughing extremely loudly. Nonstop laughing, with his head pointed at the ceiling like he was going mad. Then he suddenly saw a light shining through the basement window that was facing the street. He quickly peeped; it was the detectives—they had brought Sandra back home.

Tyler was now panicking and started spraying the bug spray to get the scent of the blood away; he peeped again, and he heard his mom saying.

"This will not end like this, I will get a lawyer, and I will fight this. I will go to the *Daily Lemon* if I have to," said Sandra.

"I'm sorry for your loss, Ms. Cook, and I support your decision," said the detective.

"Mmmhmm, by the way, I didn't get your name," Sandra said.

"It's Detective Joe Zimmerman," he said.

Sandra then went inside her house. The detectives were now leaving as well. Then Detective Zimmerman suddenly saw a red handprint on the back of Sandra's car trunk.

"Is that blood?" he asked the other detective. The other detective then looked at it.

"It's probably just a sticker. Sandra is a registered nurse; it's probably some cancer awareness stuff," he said.

They got in the car and drove off, with Tyler still watching all of this from the window.

And as he watched them leave, without any fear on Tyler's face, he stood at the basement window, looked through, and said,

"REST IN PEACE, TONY WHITTAKER. ONLY 10 MORE TO GO!"

[THE MAN WITH THE BLACK HEARSE]

1970—crime was plaguing all of Lennord County. Organized crime controlled the whole city. Every night there was another burning building, another car bombing, and another businessman getting killed for not paying extortion; often, local residents could see bodies floating above the Hudson River. The F.B.I. couldn't seem to get a handle on Lennord County's crimewave, thus leaving the county to the Mafia to do whatever they felt the need to do. The Mafia had judges, lawyers, and the entire police force in their pockets; they controlled the restaurants, the fish business, and even the docks. They flooded the streets with cocaine and racketeering, just murder after murder. Almost every funeral home in the county was overbooked with work: one man, in particular, had a lot of business coming in—we are speaking of the funeral director, Steven Lamb.

Steven Lamb, a local funeral director, owned three funeral homes in the county; he had one at 100 Maine Street, Sage Town, one on 18 John Street, which was a three-minute walk from the Maine Street funeral home, and one in King Town, close to the Gettys' House. If you had a loved one who had passed away, this was the man to go to, for Steven tended to dress his dead in expensive wear and rich perfume. He was a 6-foot 2-inch tall white man, age 69, with a skinny body type, bony face, short blonde hair, no beard, no mustache, wore a black three-piece suit, with a black button down, and black bowtie; but what really stood out the most was the shiny black hearse Steven drove everywhere he went, even to the grocery store, with his wife, Connie Lamb, who was a 65-year-old, skinny black woman, 5 feet 7 inches tall, with Afro hair, hazel eyes, bony face, high cheekbones, and who dressed like a churchgoer. She worked with Steven—her job was to bathe the dead, and she was extremely in love with her husband and would do anything for him.

It was MARCH 1970.

The Mafia lifestyle was dying down, and the cops were coming down hard on organized crime with a new act called the R.I.C.O LAW. Law professor G. Robert Blakey was the one who created the law, which stands for the Racketeer, Influenced and Corrupt Organization Act. The law was put into the Act of 1970 by Richard M. Nixon himself. While this was working for the C.I.A, and while they clamped down on a lot of crime families all over New York City, there was one family that was still running shit—the Marco Crime Family.

THE MARCO CRIME FAMILY runs the entire County with extortion and prostitution; they had a cut in almost every single business place in Lennord County, from laundromats to hospitals to restaurants and even disco clubs. You could always spot a Marco family member by just his waffle weave pants, button shirt, Jesus pieces, and greased hair. The head of the family was Dante Marco, a six-foot tall Italian man with a heavy Italian/New York accent; he wore nothing but expensive Gucci suits, greased hair pressed flat and backward, no beard, a thick mustache, and smoked a cigar all the time. He hardly made a public appearance, and not even the LCPD, knew what he looked like; all they heard was the story of him. Dante had a very calm temper but was merciless when it came to his money and business. No one in Lennord County would dare to cross the Marco crime family unless you wanted to end up with your feet and hands cut off. How did he maintain such an organization, you might ask?

Dante's family was very well structured; you see, Dante was the big boss, and everyone called him Godfather. Below the Godfather were his sons, Angelo and Gabriel, their titles were called upper bosses, then below Angelo and Gabriel were ten different captains, five captains each, and below the ten captains were a whole lot of workers who had never ever even seen the boss before.

Angelo was the spitting image of his dad, just younger. He was reckless and did what he felt like. Gabriel, on the other hand, looked like his mom, with a low fade haircut. He also wore suits, graduated from Nepa University with a business degree, and he was the chief advisor for his dad, always by his dad's side; he was also responsible for the financial affairs of the business, thus explaining the reason they never paid taxes.

Dante owned a brothel, providing underground prostitution for Lennord County's horny Italian men, men who are always cheating on their wives—yes, the Mafia cheats on their wives a lot, always partying and fucking these prostitutes. At the time, prostitution was illegal in Lennord County; Dante normally got his girls imported from exotic countries, just any type of woman Lennord County hardly saw. Business was going very well for the Mafia boss. Cops were paid off; lawyers were bought out; the Marco Crime Family was running the place under one order. The family was untouchable; no one there stood in their way, well, except for one family, the Luigi Crime Family, who got jealous of the Marco family, and decided they wanted the good life also. So, they crafted a plan to take down the Marco family.

It was 10 YEARS LATER – 1980. TIME: 3 AM. LOCATION: MIDTOWN.

Angelo Marco lay dead in the street of Midtown; his car was blown up after trying to enter it. This hit was put out by the head of the Luigi Crime Family, Rocco Luigi, who had a similar setup to Marco's family. The only thing the Godfather had over Rocco was more manpower, more businesses, and more high-powered weapons.

War was in the air, for the LCNS newsgroup had already covered the story; on the morning news, we all know nothing stays silent for too long in Lennord county, and just like that, the news had reached Marco's Family. Let us take a visit to the estate.

SAGE TOWN GLASCO, THE MARCO FAMILY ESTATE, 10 AM

The big white mansion had a big pool in front, five palm trees on both sides, 15 bedrooms, seven downstairs, the rest upstairs, four bathrooms, two living rooms, one dining area, two maids, one butler, and a secret underground den, where the Godfather conducted all his business. Let us go straight to the Godfather's Den—brown door with European carving, polished board walls, and four moose heads in all four corners. The room was poorly lit, with a red Persian carpet lying on the floor; in the middle is a big round table, with four chairs around it, with three Italian mobsters. The Godfather was sitting in front, Gabriel beside him, and the other guy was standing at the door, keeping guard. Gabriel then got up and looked at the empty chair where Angelo should be.

"Godfather, we have bad news," said Gabriel.

"I already know," said the Godfather.

"That fucking Luigi family; let's kill all of them," said the guard at the door.

"Angelo knows not to leave without an escort," said the Godfather while he fed the fish in an aquarium below the table.

"It has to be Rocco and his dogs, thinking they all are fucking wise guys," said Gabriel. Dante then got up, put the fish food down on the table, and went by what seemed to be a secret liquor stash. He then grabbed a bottle of whiskey, poured three glasses, and handed two to Gabriel and the other guy.

"We need to act now, boss," said the bodyguard.

"Yes, but let us properly bury my son," said the Godfather.

"Gather everyone in the main living room; I will tell the news," he further said.

Moments later, Gabriel had congregated everyone in the main living room, over 50 people dressed in black suits, women in expensive fur coats, smoking cigarettes, and kids running around with fake guns, playing cops and robber, or better yet, cops and Mafia, nonstop Italian chattery, maids and butler hard at work, serving food and drinks, it was strictly Italian dishes. You could hear the sound of eggs mixing in metal pans, and oven doors going back and forth, while the loud chattery continues, Dante then walked in, and everyone who had been sitting down was now standing up.

"GODFATHER, GODFATHER, GODFATHER, GODFATHER."

One by one, they all greeted Dante.

"Please sit down," said Dante; they all sat back down. His wife Sofia then walked over to him; she hugged and kissed him.

Sofia Marco, 52 years old, lazy, spends most of her time shopping and wasting Dante's money; black curly hair, sexy body, high cheekbones, and blue eyes, wears nothing but expensive fur coats over her, all in one dress, cut right above her knee, very clean skin, no blemishes, the woman knows how to take care of herself, rich perfume, high heels, and drives a Cadillac.

The Godfather then spoke.

"I have some bad news; Angelo lost his life this morning in Midtown, on route 211," he said. Everyone was looking all confused, and his wife looked at him.

"What are you talking about, Dan?" Sofia asked him as she moderately broke down to sob.

"His car was blown to shreds," said the Godfather. Sofia started crying, "No, not Angelo," she said. "Not my Angelo." Sofia then fainted.

"Come get your mother," said the Godfather to Gabriel.

"Godfather is it the Luigi Family?" one member of the family asked.

"Unfortunately, it is," said Dante.

Then suddenly, all the Mob members pulled their Tommy machine guns from under their long tuxedo trench coats.

"Everyone, calm down!" said the Godfather. Moments later, they all came to a halt but still mumbled.

"EVERYONE, CALM DOWN!" Gabriel shouted. Then suddenly, everyone calmed down.

"Go ahead, Godfather," he further said.

"Whether or not it's the Luigi family, we will do nothing until I bury my son," said the Godfather.

"The wake will be in two days at St. Michael's Church in Glasco," he further said.

Moments later, the Godfather had dispatched the Mob to their usual errands—you know, the extortion, the debt collection, the running of the brothel.

Everyone then scattered.

The Godfather, Gabriel, and Sofia were now in Angelo's room, making funeral arrangements. The bodyguard was standing outside the room door.

Sofia was sitting on his bed; she took her fur coat off, and Gabriel sat beside her,

"How could you make him leave on his own, Gabriel?" Sofia asked her son.

"No one can tell Angelo what to do, ma," he replied.

"Oh! Don't give me that bullshit," said Sofia as she pulled out a cigarette and crossed her legs.

"You two are responsible for this," she further said as she looked at Dante with scorn.

"Enough, Sofia. As a matter of fact, why don't you go wait for me outside? I need to talk to Gabriel alone," said the Godfather.

Sofia screamed, then she got up, put the cigarette back in the box, she started walking. Dante grabbed her arms, pulled her in, put his mouth to her ears.

"Rocco will die for this," he said. She then turned around, facing him, Dante, just inches away.

"You better," she said; she pushed him off and walked out of the room,

Dante then looked at his son. "He needs to get the best funeral," said the Godfather.

"Who should we use?" the Godfather asked Gabriel.

"Why don't you use Mr. Lamb? He is just around the corner," said Gabriel.

"Who is that?" asked the Godfather asked.

"He lives in the town of Sage Town," said Gabriel.

"He owns three funeral homes in all of Lennord county," said Gabriel. The Godfather then paused and looked at Gabriel with a semi-stern face.

"Does he pay extortion?" he asked.

"Godfather, no one ever thought of taxing a death house," said Gabriel.

"Wise guy, huh!" said the Godfather. "Well, it's settled; call Lamb," he further said.

Moments later, Gabriel called Mr. Lamb; he took the job. But after telling his wife he was doing a funeral service for the Marco Crime Family, Connie told him to decline the job and not work for them "They are bad people," she said.

TUESDAY, 1980. THE DAY OF ANGELO'S WAKE

St. Michael's Church was full of Italians in black three-piece suits, long trench coats, and greased hair; Angelo was lying dead in his casket, and Sofia was crying up a storm while she looked at his heavily made-up face with stitches under it.

Mr. Lamb had done a great job of putting Angelo back together, given how badly the bomb had ripped his face off. Steven was now standing at the church's door as he watched everyone crying and grieving for the deceased. Inside was Dante; he saw Steven standing by himself, and he walked towards him moments later.

"Mr. Lamb," said the Godfather.

"To what do I owe this pleasure?" said Steven.

"Impressive work, you did, indeed, stitching Angelo's face back together," said the Godfather.

"Thank you, and I'm sorry for your loss, Mr. Marco," said Steven.

"People die daily, Mr. Lamb; what makes my son special?" he asked. "I heard that you own three funeral homes in my county?" the Godfather further asked Steven, Steven now looking a little scared now, as he spoke.

"Yes, Mr. Marco," said Mr. Lamb.

"Mr. Lamb, I heard you don't pay a protection fee," said the Godfather,

"What do you mean, Mr. Marco?" asked Mr. Lamb.

"You know!" he said. "That money you need to pay every month for living in my county," said the Godfather. Dante then looked at Lamb with a cynical look.

"I want no trouble, Mr. Marco," said Steven.

"So, you do understand; I run this place, Mr. Lamb?" he asked Steven.

"Yes, Mr. Marco," said Steven.

"There only one man I allow to live rent-free in my city, and that is Mr. Andre Paul, and no one else," said the Godfather, "Do you know who Andre Paul is, Mr. Lamb?" the Godfather asked Steven as he stepped closer to him.

"Yes, Mr. Marco," he replied.

"Do you know why I give him that privilege, Mr. Lamb?" the Godfather asked.

"No, Mr. Marco," he said.

"Back in 1976, some of my men were carrying out a regular extortion; they got to the Dailey Lemon to extort Mr. Andre Paul. When my man got there and asked him for the money, you know what he did, Mr. Lamb?" the Godfather asked.

"No, Mr. Marco," Steven replied.

"He gave them an unreleased book written by him and said, 'Give this to Mr. Dante Marco and tell him to extort some damn knowledge.' My men had genuinely respected his bravery; they took his book and brought it back to me, and Mr. Lamb, that book is now locked up in my safe; no one else reads it but me," said the Godfather.

"Do you know why I told you that story, Mr. Lamb?" the Godfather asked Steven.

"Not sure, Mr. Marco," he replied.

"Mr. Lamb, in order to live free in my county, you need to offer something of value, just like Mr. Andre Paul," said the Godfather. "Mr. Lamb, you will be called upon to perform duties from time to time if I need to bury someone again," Dante further said; he then walked away.

Steven then stepped out and quickly got in his black hearse; he then decided to sit there for the rest of the wake. Upon sitting, he noticed two men sitting in a black car with cameras, taking pictures of the entire Marco Family; he paid no mind to it.

About half an hour later, everyone was now making their way out, getting into their respective vehicles. Steven was now putting the casket in the black hearse; everyone was driving off, black car after black car, off to the burial ground to lay Angelo to rest.

R.I.P Angelo Marco

ASHES TO ASHES, DUST TO DUST

And just like that, Angelo 'Dante' Marco was laid to rest.

5 DAYS LATER

Again, in the Den, Dante, and Gabriel were back in business mode, ready to pick up where they left off, with vengeance on their minds, ice in their hearts, and fire in their eyes.

"Godfather, it's now time for new imports," said Gabriel.

"Where to this time?" the Godfather asked.

"Peru," said Gabriel.

"I have made a connection in Peru to have 30 Peruvian women imported back to Lennord County by ship; travel will be 2 to 3 weeks," said Gabriel.

"Okay, and what do we do in the meantime?" the Godfather asked.

"Revenge for Angelo," said Gabriel while he looked at his dad.

The Marco family had decided to kill the entire Luigi Crime Family.

"I want you to bomb their houses, their cars, business places, spare no one," said the Godfather.

"Actually, I have a smoother idea, Godfather," said Gabriel.

"Oh? And what is that?" he asked.

"Let us kill them one by one and have Mr. Lamb burn the bodies; that way, nothing leads back to us. I want to change the dynamic of war; no more outbursts, let us move in silence," said Gabriel.

"That may be the best Idea I have heard," said the Godfather. "Where do we begin?" he further asked.

"We already have eyes on all ten of Rocco's captains," said Gabriel.

The Godfather then looked at his son, smiled, and nodded his head.

"KILL THEM ALL," he said.

It was a bloody operation; the Marco Crime Family was successful, murder after murder, members of the Luigi Crime Family went missing, and one by one, Steven Lamb burned the bodies of Rocco's crew.

They were triumphant, even though they had lost a lot of manpower in the process.

THREE WEEKS LATER

Back at the Den again, it was now 7 p.m. in the evening. Gabriel and his dad were sitting around the table, having a drink and watching the news.

The news anchors spoke:

Good day Lennord County, It's been three weeks since the disappearance of the entire Luigi family, leaving Rocco Luigi, all alone in his mansion in King Town. What a bizarre case. The question the entire county is asking is, where could they all have gone? Did they all go back to Italy? he asked sarcastically.

Gabriel then turned the TV off; his phone rang, and he answered,

"Hey boss, the shipment has arrived," said the person on the phone. Gabriel looked at his dad. He then spoke.

"Okay, you and ten more guys, guard the docks and do not touch any of the women; the boss and I will be there soon," said Gabriel. Gabriel and Dante then grabbed their coats and went to the main living room, where most of the men were already waiting for orders.

Moments later, Dante and half of the Mafia, along with Gabriel, all headed to the docks with big trucks to go get the girls. They got to the dock, and there was no sound coming from the boat. Gabriel then tried to call his guy, but there was no answer. They got closer and realized all 11 men were dead.

All their throats were cut. They quickly climbed aboard; the captain was dead as well.

"What is going on?" the Godfather asked.

They quickly rushed to the lower quarters; the lights were off, and an awful scent hit them. Dante stepped down and stepped into something liquid,

"Can I get some fucking light?" he shouted. Gabriel struck his lighter.

A surprise—all 30 Peruvian women were swimming dead in their own blood.

"What the fuck is this?" said the Godfather.

They took a closer look; each female had about three shots to the head. Dante was now panicking, looking at Gabriel for answers.

"Thirty dead Peruvian women, Godfather; how will we explain this to the cops?" Gabriel asked.

"What should we do?" he asked.

"Call Steven Lamb," said the Godfather. Gabriel looked at his dad; he did not hesitate.

Gabriel then rang Steven; it rang out, no answer; he tried again, but still no answer.

"Who, you think, did this?" Gabriel asked. "You think it was the Luigi family?" he further asked.

"No, I don't think so; Rocco doesn't kill women," said the Godfather.

"Then who could've done this? This is inhumane," said Gabriel.

"Let us go pay Mr. Lamb a visit," said the Godfather. Dante, Gabriel, and the rest of the Mafia were now making their way out; they got outside, and this was when they all heard:

"**Dante Julius Marco**, you and the rest of the family are all under arrest for the murder of 30 Peruvian women. You have the right to remain silent; anything you say or do could be used against you in a court of law," said one of the F.B.I. officers. The SWAT team was there, and so were the paramedics. And just like that, the entire Marco family was arrested on several counts of R.I.C.O charges. The entire Marco family got 65 to life, and Rocco died from a rare illness.

The Mafia lifestyle had now come to an end.

ONE MONTH LATER

And the streets of Lennord County were no longer full of gang violence, both the Marco and Luigi crime family no longer existed, and the County celebrated their disappearance and praised the F.B.I.

Allan Sharp, director of the F.B.I. agency, was awarded a medal of honor and was a national hero for taking down two of the most notorious Italian crime families. Allan Sharp worked on this case for years. Watching this from his funeral home TV was none other than Steven Lamb.

He was sitting in his office on John Street, crying and weeping, with a rope in his hand and a note in his pocket. He got up, tossed the rope over the ceiling bar, tied it firmly, placed a chair below the rope, and put his neck between the rope. Then he kicked the chair. Unfortunately, Steven Lamb hanged himself and couldn't bear the pressure of burning all those bodies for the Mafia. There he swung when suddenly his wife stepped in and saw Steven dead in his office.

She instantly got confused; it was so sudden to her. She did not scream; she was just standing there trembling. She started to cry. "Why Steven?" she asked herself, she then saw the note in his pocket; she took the note out, she realized the note was addressed to her, she opened the note, her eyes were wide opened as she read, she started crying again, as she continued to read. The note read,

"HEY, CONNIE LAMB, IF YOU ARE READING THIS, THAT MEANS I MUST BE DEAD; I SHOULD'VE LISTENED TO YOU AND NEVER TAKEN THAT JOB. I'M SORRY, BUT DANTE WASN'T THE ONE WHO KILLED THOSE PERUVIAN WOMEN, IT WAS THE F.B.I. DIRECTOR ALLAN SHARP, THE F.B.I. ORCHESTRATED THE WHOLE THING. THEY KILLED ALL 30 WOMEN TO FRAME DANTE MARCO. PLEASE TAKE THIS TO THE LENNORD COUNTY NEWS STATION."

[THE BLEACHER]

Aliyah Smith was a 12-year-old girl with melanin darker than space, standing about 5 feet 3 inches tall, with braided hair, a slim face, skinny body, blue eyes, wearing mostly pajamas when she was home, but a green button blouse and khaki skirt when she was at school. Aliyah attended the King Town Middle School, which is right across from the Gettys house. She has two friends, Lisa and Latanya (Latty for short), white twins from Glasco, Sage Town. Aaliyah lives with her mom, Kahlia Wright, on the outskirts of King Town. Kahlia is a stay-in nurse who spends most of her Saturdays and Sundays attending to an old lady named Agatha Mills. Agatha lived four blocks away from Kahlia's house, so getting there was no hard travel, just a short walk. Kahlia, standing at 6 feet, was a very tall black woman with a slim upper body, big butt, and thick thighs; you should see when she wears her scrubs, she busts them panties wide open. She has a male haircut, which she maintains at her local barber. Thursday nights were when she got her edge-ups and the rest of the week she spent with Aliyah. It was

JULY 2000 – WARM AS HELL

This was the year Aliyah had come to hate her lovely dark melanin due to the constant viewing of a white woman on TV. Aliyah enjoyed watching "Real Housewives of Lennord County." She normally watched this show when Kahlia was at Agatha's for the weekend, and because it was just four blocks away, Kahlia tended not to check on Aliyah. Aliyah got caught up with this show, which consisted of only white women, talking all sorts of nonsense and spending their husband's money on all types of fuckery. After a month of watching the show, Aliyah started to think that a clearer skin was more attractive than darker skin, and from then on, she started to use her mom's makeup.

But to be honest, do you think a TV show full of only white women could really be enough to convince a 12-year-old black girl that white skin was better?

Well, the answer is No! It's not that simple. Now let us visit back to where Aliyah's journey for a clearer skin all began.

JUNE 2000. A BRIGHT SUNNY DAY. 85 DEGREES.

King Town Middle School was in session, and hundreds of students, wearing dark green and khaki colors, were rushing for class; but let us visit Aliyah's classroom.

The classroom had 21 kids, separated into seven benches, with three students per bench. Sitting in the fifth row was Aliyah, to her left was Latty, and to the right was Lisa, the rich twins whose parents owned two Price Choppers in Sage Town, just off 32.

Aliyah, Lisa, and Latty were friends and spent every recess together at the jungle gym, where they hung out and talked about a lot of stuff.

Before we go any further, here is the thing about these three: see, even though they were just 12 years old, the three tended to always find themselves indulging in real grown-up types of arguments. They weren't afraid to say it all.

IT WAS NOW 11:55 AM

"It's five minutes before recess; what do you guys want to do for the next 30 minutes?" said Latty.

Standing 5 feet 4 inches tall, a skinny white girl with short blonde hair and black eyes, dressed in her green blouse and khaki skirt, Latty was an independent personality; she didn't follow the crowd on who to be friends with.

"What do you mean? We are going by the gym like we always do," said Lisa. "I want to tell you guys something so badly," she further said, while she looked at Aliyah staring out a space.

Lisa looked like Latanya but with a very mature woman-type personality who was not afraid to talk about adult sexual content.

THE BELL RANG. IT WAS NOW TIME FOR RECESS.

Aliyah, Lisa, and Latty all rushed to the jungle gym; some students were all sitting there, and they all walked up.

"You guys need to fucking leave; this is our spot," said Lisa as she kicked the chip woods at the other students; the other students didn't even retaliate; they all got up and walked away like pussies.

"You can take it easy sometimes," said Aliyah to Lisa, but Lisa ignored her. They all sat down, and Aliyah started to kick the chipped wood.

"Hey Aliyah, did you see Mr. Keen's dick pressing out in his pants?" said Lisa as she smiled.

"Could we not talk about that, please?" said Latty.

"What, it's big, isn't it?" Lisa asked. Aliyah seemed standoffish about the conversation.

"Aliyah, what is wrong? Did your cherry get popped?" Lisa further said.

"Can we have one day where we don't talk about any sexual stuff? We are still just 12; you know that, right?" said Latty.

"So what?" said Lisa. "If no one can hear us speak, how are they going to know we said it?" she further said. She continued to talk. "Furthermore, if everything is on social media, and our parents let us watch whatever we want to watch, how can you blame me for wanting to talk about Mr. Keen's big dick?" said 12-year-old Lisa Miller.

"Still," said Latty, "And you are wrong; Aliyah's mom doesn't make her watch everything," said Latty.

"Aliyah watches Real Housewives of Lennord County," said Lisa.

"She has to hide and watch it," said Latty.

"My point exactly; she is watching adult stuff behind her mom's back," said Lisa.

"The same thing I'm doing right now," she further said.

"Whatever, Lisa," said Latty.

"Guys, am I too black?" Aliyah asked; the twins then stared at her with a confused look.

"No! Of course not," said Lisa.

"That is how I know you are lying," said Aliyah. "Because you damn well know I'm super black," she further said.

"Okay, but why are you asking this?" Lisa asked.

"Nothing, forget it," said Aliyah.

Thirty minutes later, recess had come to an end, and students were now back in class, getting ready for the last lap of the day; the usual process where teachers teach, and students pretend to learn.

School went on until about 3 pm in the afternoon.

The bell rang, and the big yellow buses were already parked outside, waiting for pickups; students were now busting through the big doors, rushing towards the buses. One by one, they climbed aboard. The majority of the school rode the buses, and that included Aliyah as well.

There she stood on the outside, waving bye to Lisa and Latty while they got in their mother's expensive Jaguar car.

"Bye, Ali," said Latty and Lisa.

"Bye, guys," Aliyah replied, then headed for the bus; Lisa and Latty then drove off.

Lisa and Latty were now making their way to their mansion in Glasco; they merged onto 9W.

"Are you guys friends with that black girl?" asked Tammy, the mother of the twins. She then looked at them through her rearview mirror.

Tammy, a very sexy white woman, a brunette with a skinny face and high cheekbones, acted like she was better than everyone who was not as rich as her. She has a short temper—her husband left her for another woman, and she secretly disliked black people but kept it to herself.

"Yes, Mommy, Aliyah is our friend," said Lisa with a whispery tone.

Now if you notice, Lisa's tone had changed. That is because she was afraid of her mother and worked hard to get her attention. Latty, on the other hand, didn't fear her mom and would stand up to her when she got the chance, but Tammy would slap Latty in the face if she backtalked too much.

"I see, but she is so," said Tammy—and paused for a second.

"So black, is that what you are afraid to say?" said Latty.

"Isn't there anyone else in school you guys could make friends with?" Tammy asked.

"Mom, why would you ask that?" Latty asked her mom.

"I ask whatever I want to ask Latty," she said to Latty with a stern face.

"Lisa, how close are you with this girl?" she asked Lisa. "You sure you like her?" she further asked.

Moments after getting home, Latty didn't speak to anyone. She got out of the car, bolted into the house, said hi to the maid, went straight to her room, got on her bed, and instantly called Aliyah to have their usual girl talk after school.

She dialed (845) 456-8888.

"Hey, girl," said Aliyah.

If you noticed, Aliyah's tone of voice had shifted to a calmer and lighter tone; that is because there was a different chemistry between those two.

"What are you doing, girl?" Latty asked.

"That homework Mr. Keen gave us, and waiting for my mom to get home," said Aliyah.

"Oh yeah, am a do it in the morning," said Latty. "Anyway, my family had pissed me off, so not in the mood for them," said Latty.

"What happened?" Aliyah asked.

"Hold on, Ali, Lisa is calling me; let me call you back, Al," she said. Aliyah hung up and then went back to doing her homework: Social Studies.

She needed to write about a time she contributed to society by helping someone in need of help. She wrote about a time she visited Agatha and helped her mom to bathe her.

Moments later, Kahlia was now getting home from the barbershop. She parked around the back of the house under a big tree.

She went into the house, walked to the back door, and called out for Aliyah.

"Aliyah baby, can you come help me with these bags, please," she said.

"Coming, Mom," she replied. Aliyah quickly jumped out of bed and went into the living room and walked through the front door.

"Honey, I'm in the back," said Kahlia. She quickly turned around and headed for the kitchen; through the back door she went.

"Please be careful with the meat," she said.

"Okay, Mom," she said.

She then grabbed the other bags and noticed there was ground beef in this already ripped brown paper bag.

"Ground beef again," she said to herself.

She then grabbed the bag and went back in; she closed the back door.

"Mommy, please don't park on the grass again," she said to her mom.

"Okay, and why is that, Aliyah?" Kahlia asked.

"I sleep on the grass sometimes," she said.

"Okay but be careful because that grass is full of all types of insects," she replied.

Thirty minutes later…

Kahlia was now cooking; Aliyah was in her pajamas, sitting in the living room, deleting all the prerecorded episodes of "The Real Housewives of Lennord County," she had been hiding from her mom.

You see, Kahlia was pro-black and strongly believed that black people were forever oppressed, and black oppression was the reason for her poverty and single-mom life.

"What are you watching, honey?" she asked Aliyah.

"Waiting to Exhale," she replied.

"Who stars in that movie?" she asked.

"Angela Bassett, Whitney Houston, Loretta Devine, and Lela Rochon," Aliyah replied.

"Oh, that is a great mix of black women," Kahlia said. "I'm proud of how much you are into your black culture," she further said as she finished up with the cooking.

"Mom, are all white people rich?" Aliyah asked her mom. Kahlia stopped what she was doing and looked at her daughter. "I don't think so," she said.

"Are there more rich white people than blacks?" she asked.

"Most definitely," said Kahlia. "But honey let us not talk about this right now," she abruptly said, then went back to cooking.

Twenty minutes later...

Kahlia now joined Aliyah with tacos for dinner; they watched the movie together, and after that, they went to bed. She slept beside her mom that night.

FRIDAY MORNING

Aliyah was now off to school. She took the yellow bus, which took longer this time, but nonetheless, it got her to school on time; she was now walking to class as she looked at everyone. Upon walking, Aliyah gazed away, looking at all the white kids that attended King Town Middle School. She looked left—she saw two white girls with expensive bags and shoes. She looked right—she saw four poor black students at the water dispenser, counting coins. She then looked right again—she saw seven rich white boys with their expensive gadgets showing off. She then entered her classroom; she saw Lisa and Latty already sitting,

"Hey, guys," she said, but only Latty answered.

"Aliyah said hello, Lisa," said Latty as she stared at her sister.

"I'm not obligated to answer her," said Lisa.

"What is your problem, can't see Mrs. Lesley's dick," said Aliyah.

Lisa gave her a dirty stare. "Whatever blackie," said Lisa. Aliyah looked at Lisa intensely.

"No, for real; what is your problem, yo," said Aliyah. She then sat down.

"Latty, can I switch places with you?" Lisa asked.

"Sure, whatever," she replied. Lisa then switched places with Latty.

Latty was now the mediator for Lisa and Aliyah as she sat between them.

For the entire class session, Lisa and Aliyah did not speak to each other.

RECESS AGAIN

Aliyah and Latty were the only ones sitting alone at the jungle gym. Lisa didn't show up.

LAST BELL

Lisa didn't tell Aliyah bye. She walked past her, got in her mom's car, and held her head straight.

Aliyah told Latty bye and headed for the bus. "Have a great weekend, Latty," she said as she ran to the bus.

Moments later, Aliyah got home, same as usual, with ground beef dinner and a note from her mom.

"Honey, Agatha isn't feeling well. I had to come in today. Dinner is already on the stove. See you Sunday," the note said.

She then had dinner, watched her TV show, and went straight to bed.

A new day came.

SATURDAY MORNING. 10 AM

Aliyah was all by herself, her mom still at Agatha's. She made breakfast, milk, and cereal, and she started watching "Real Housewives of Lennord County." There she sat, Indian style, in front of the TV; her phone rang. It was Lisa; she ignored it. It rang again; this time, it was Latty. She smiled and answered.

"What's up, girl?" she said.

"This is not Latty, you little bitch!" said Lisa. "I was just calling you to tell you, please don't talk to me when you see me at school on Monday," she further said.

"Fine, whatever, Lisa," said Aliyah and hung up.

She then waited four minutes and then called Latty. Latty answered.

"What is her problem?" she asked Latty.

"It was something mom told her," Latty replied.

"Does your mom hate me? She gave me this bad look yesterday," Aliyah asked Latty.

"My mom probably hates herself," said Latty. "Don't pay this any mind," she further said. "Anyway, what are you doing? Watching Real Housewives of Lennord County?" she asked

"How did you know?" she said and smiled.

"You always watch that stupid shit with all of them fake-ass white bitches," she said to Aliyah.

"They are so fancy and rich; I love seeing them," Aliyah replied.

"Okay, weirdo, but I will catch up with you later," she said and then hung up.

Aliyah then went back to watching her show. Then suddenly, an ad came on. A bald-headed white man, dressed in a three-piece grey suit with a blue button down and pink tie, started talking. He said:

"DO YOU THINK YOU ARE TOO DARK? DO YOUR FRIENDS CALL YOU BLACK? IF SO, I HAVE JUST THE THING FOR YOU. THIS RIGHT HERE, THIS IS THE MAGIC CREAM, ONE RUB, AND YOU WILL BE WHITE AS SNOW. IT IS THAT SIMPLE. IF YOU FEEL NUMBNESS, PLEASE CONTACT YOUR DOCTOR. YOU MUST BE 18 AND OLDER TO ORDER,"

Aliyah quickly wrote the number down. The TV then switched back to the Housewives of Lennord County.

There she sat, watching and listening keenly to what the ladies were talking about when one of the women suddenly asked a complicated question to the rest of the Housewives.

"Name one black man you would date?" she asked all nine of the other middle-aged white women.

"Idris Elba," said one woman.

"Damian Marley," said another woman.

"Denzel Washington," said another woman.

"Vybz Kartel," said another woman.

"Shabba Ranks," said another woman.

"Samuel Jackson," said another woman.

"Patrick Gaynor," said another woman.

"Jay-Jay Okocha," said another woman.

"How about you," they asked a woman who appeared to be a guest on today's show.

"Who me?" she asked.

"Yes, which black man are you into?" they asked her.

"Oh, I'm only into one black, and that is my husband," she said.

"Who is that?" the Housewives asked her.

"jlawremone," she said.

"Come on, there must be another black man you find sexy," they said.

"Nope, not for me," she said.

Then the ad suddenly came back on.

"IF BLACK IS NOT YOUR COLOR OF CHOICE, WHY NOT UPGRADE TO A SNOW-LIKE DESIGN? YOU SEE, WHEN YOU ARE WHITE, YOUR PRIVILEGES ARE BRIGHT." Said the man in the Ad.

The ad then cut off; Aliyah was now intrigued by this cream, and she schemed and planned. She then took her mom's credit card and ordered the "Magic Cream," online; she ordered the next-day shipping.

NEXT DAY-SUNDAY MORNING.

The package arrived, but her mom was still at Agatha's; Aliyah collected the package without her mum knowing. She opened the package and took out. It was a black tube, like a toothpaste tube, and said, "Magic Cream," in a white font.

Aliyah read the directions and warnings.

Direction: apply just a fingertip of cream. Spread all over the face. Avoid eyes. Stay in a shaded area till the cream dissolves.

Warning: IF YOU FEEL NUMBNESS, PLEASE STOP, WIPE CREAM OFF FACE, AND CONTACT YOUR DOCTOR.

Her phone rang. It was Kahlia. She answered.

"Hey, mom," she said.

"Are you okay?" she asked. Agatha spoke. "Is that my beautiful blueberry pie?" Agatha asked Kahlia. Agatha was another senile old pro-black woman.

"Yes, mom, just watching TV," said Aliyah,

"Mrs. Reed said hi," said Kahlia.

"Tell her I said hi," she replied.

"She says your black is astounding," she said.

"Mommy, quick question, why did dad leave?" she asked her abruptly.

"Why are you asking this baby?" she asked.

"Did he leave you for a white woman?" she asked Kahlia. "Do black men prefer white women?" she further asked.

"Aliyah, we will talk about this later," she replied with a sternness in her voice.

"Okay," she said. Aliyah then quickly looked at her phone. She was getting another call. It was Latty.

She let it ring out.

"Mom, I will see you later," she said, then hung up. Now she hurried up to return Latty's call.

As she was about to dial, she saw that Latty had already left her a voice message.

She pressed play, and Latty started talking,

"Hey Aliyah, you were right, my mom doesn't like you, and I know why. So, I overheard her telling Lisa that dad had left her for a black woman, and that is why she doesn't like black people but pays that no mind. I like you, Aliyah; I love your black skin. Anyway, how is your Sunday going?" Latty asked.

Then in the background, you could hear Lisa talking, "Is that Aliyah? Hey bitch, all your people good for stealing other people, man," she said.

"Could you not do that, Lisa?" said Latty.

"Why are you still friends with her?" Lisa asked Latty.

"Because I can be myself around Aliyah, and she is way more of a sister than you," she said to Lisa.

"Be honest, don't you think Aliyah is maaaad! UGLY?" said Lisa.

The voice message ended. Aliyah started crying.

Aliyah quickly went to the bathroom, grabbed the Magic Cream, and because she was crying in rage, she unconsciously applied half of the tube of Magic Cream on her face, totally ignoring the directions. She looked into the mirror as tears ran down her face.

"I will be clear and pretty," she said.

She then went back into the living room and sat down, feet folded, in her pajamas. Minutes later, she decided to go into the backyard and take a nap under the big tree, where the swing was. She was now about to turn the TV off, for the show was still on, she then heard.

"Andre Paul," said the guest on the show.

"Who is Andre Paul?" the host of the show asked the guest,

"The other black guy that I admire a lot," said the guest on the show.

"Who is Andre Paul?" they asked.

"He is this local writer who lives in Sage Town," said the guest.

Aliyah turned the TV off. Then hissed her teeth.

"STUPID WHITE BITCHES," she said.

"Ann Taylor is just tricking y'all. Andre Paul is also jlawremone," Aliyah further said to herself as she made her way to the backyard.

"Mommy really knows every black man's business in this county," said Aliyah. The product was now hardened up on her face.

She headed to the big tree. She lay on the grass, smiling, thinking that her light skin was about to come any minute now. Aliyah fell asleep, snoring loudly. The back door constantly swung from the dry wind; she was knocked out under the cool shades. Minutes passed by. You could see Aliyah's body as she lay comfortably with the Magic Cream on her face.

Then suddenly, worms started to crawl from the earth and gathered close to Aliyah. About 50 black parasitic worms were crawling towards Aliyah. While she snored heavily, the worms finally got to her. The worms were now bundled up in Aliyah's palm. It looked like they were eating the cream from her hands. She was still sleeping while the worms crawled over each other, sticky and moist, then suddenly all the worms started to crawl to her upper body. The worms made their way to Aliyah's face; they stood still on her face for a long period of time, then they started to eat the cream from her face. Aliyah was still asleep while the worms devoured the Magic Cream.

Then out of nowhere, the worms started to dig through Aliyah's pigment. Her face started to bleed as the Black slimy worms dug through their way down, searching for more cream. Aliyah's face was extremely numb due to the excessive amount of Magic Cream used; she couldn't feel a thing. You could see the tails of the worms as they all made their way to her brain. Aliyah died in her sleep, blood leaking through her nose and ears.

Sorry to tell you, but 12-year-old Aliyah Smith was killed by 50 black parasitic worms that devoured her entire face. Aliyah was lying dead under the dark shade. Her mom was on her way home with makeup that matched her skin because she realized Aliyah had been using hers.

Aliyah's body was now full of all types of insects. As the heat from the sun penetrated her dead flesh, it started to smell. The door was still swinging from the dry air, and the TV was still on. Then suddenly, the salesman came back on.

"IF YOU THINK YOU ARE TOO WHITE, I HAVE JUST THE RIGHT THING FOR YOU. THIS, RIGHT HERE, IS THE "MAGIC TAN," ONE RUB, AND YOU WILL BE DARK AS MUD. THIS CREAM ALSO INCREASES BUTT SIZE AND INCREASES LIPS TO A FULL SIZE. PLEASE ORDER NOW, MUST BE 21 AND OLDER TO ORDER,"

[THE TOP SCAMMER]

Scamming had become a pandemic throughout the whole of Lennord County, where others were calling upon wealthy people, telling them they had won millions of dollars but needed to send a fee to clear the amount.

The Lennord County News Station recently released a press release showing a statistic of which age groups were being targeted. Statistics showed single white women between the ages of 55 to 75, white males in nursing homes between the ages of 75 to 80, and single black women who were constantly on dating websites between the ages of 50 to 60.

The News Anchor spoke.

"It looks like these scammers are targeting strictly single wealthy people," said the anchor reading the press release. "But even with this information, people are still getting random calls, and random people are still falling for the same tricks," he said again. "Lennord County, I ask you this, why are we allowing these scammers to roam free in our county? I'm asking you, Lennord County, why are we protecting these bad people? Why is no one reporting to the cops?" said the news anchor.

Peter Hush was a chubby black guy, age 40, born in Nepa Town, of Nigerian parents. Standing at 5 feet 8 inches tall, with hazel eyes, he believed in voodoo and worshiped money; he had a low fade haircut, a clean-cut beard, and owned a lot of gold chains. He wore Gucci sweats suits when out in public; he was secretly known in the street as "Top Scammer Hush." Locals from the poor part of Lennord County called him "the man," for he liked to give back to the community. You could say he knew how to get the job done, and he never failed.

Hush had three other people he worked with: his friend Calvin Blake and two females, one white, the other black. These three play a vital role in the ritual—let us look at their jobs.

Let us start with Calvin Blake, a.k.a German, who got the nickname, because of his German Ruger gun and his German knife.

Calvin Blake, age 45, just flew in from Rockfort, Jamaica. He came to spend the summer with his longtime associate Peter Hush; he stood 6 feet tall, had a heavy Jamaican accent, and said the word "Bomboclaat," on the regular during his conversations with Hush, the girls, or when he was on the phone talking to his grandma, back home. He was bald-headed and wore a red, green, and gold mesh marina tucked into his blue jeans, with one of the pants' legs folded up while the other ran down to his Desert Clarks. He had a very bad temper, and when rolling in the street with Hush, walked with a German-built knife called "The 3-star Rachet." This knife was generally German and made to open quickly and was associated with "rude boy," masculinity. Calvin was responsible for the protection of Peter Hush.

Nakeisha Barns, standing 5 feet 7 inches, with long black straight hair, a skinny face, high cheekbones, and brown eyes, was a native of Lennord County and grew up in Nepa Town and Sage Town. At age 25, she graduated from Nepa University with a B.S. in communications and a minor in theatre. "This bitch knows how to put on a show," Hush often said. She spoke fluent Spanish and occasionally showed signs of cowardness. She had dark skin and a very attractive body, always wearing business-type outfits, a black jacket, a white button-down tucked into her tight black skirt, or sometimes her tight black pants with black heels. She worked from 2 pm to 7 pm every day at the Lennord County Savings Bank in King Town and for Peter in the mornings.

She started working for Hush just after Hush had helped her with student loan debts. The two had met at Cuddy's Pub in NePa Town. She often fooled around with him, but nothing serious; her job was to play a woman manager, if need be, and to assist with Spanish clients.

Tamika Fray was a skinny blonde, white girl from Aston Villa, England, who moved to Lennord County at age 15 and was now 27. She still had her British accent but switched to New York when scamming on the phone; she was always dressed in stylish wear, and most of her clothes came from London. Her job was to source clients—how did she do this? Tamika worked at the census division in the Gettys House, where she got confidential information on everyone living in Lennord County: their names, addresses, marital status, doctor visits, etc. She then passed this information down to Nakeisha, who worked at the bank, and who, in return, matched names with income, thus generating the right clients to call upon.

You must be wondering what one of these sessions might have sounded or looked like; well, look no further. It was

MAY 2005

A big mansion was on the outskirts of Nepa Town, surrounded by a lot of woods, which made it a very quiet place; the house was sitting dormant on a hill, but looking from the north, you could see the tallest building on the campus of NEPA University. The house had a big living room, with no furniture, just a couple of chairs, with long white curtains. Upstairs was where you found all the bedrooms.

The Living Room was the room where all business was being conducted, the room where all the calls were made, and the room where all clients were tricked out of their money. Welcome to the "GUZU ROOM."

There are about 40 lit candles in a circle, two live caged chickens, a sharp knife on top of the cage, and 15 cell phones, all placed on the ground in a very neat line.

Tamika and Nakesha were both sitting on the couch, waiting for Hush and Calvin to arrive—they had gone to the local market to buy something.

Moments later, Hush and Calvin made it to the mansion. They parked around the back and decided to come in through the back door. They went in and saw the girls sitting on the chairs in the living room. It was now 10 am, and Hush and Calvin both had egg sandwiches they got from Bistro on Main Street. Hush then gave them two bags each with orange juice.

"What took you so long?" Nakesha asked.

"Calvin was hitting on this girl at Tops Supermarket," said Hush while he laughed.

"Mi know she wants the rude boy enuh," said Calvin with a Guinness in his hand and a spliff.

"Yeah, right, you had no game German," said Hush as he laughed at Calvin.

"Bwoy, watch yuh mouth, mi German a gyallis," Calvin replied; they both laughed.

"Ima get ready now," said Peter Hush as he walked upstairs, heading to his bedroom. Calvin started a conversation with Tamika; Nakesha went with Peter.

Peter, now getting ready, stripped down to his underwear. He then folded his pants and shirt, putting them on top of his bed. Nakesha then handed him a white gown with a white head cloth.

"Here you go," said Nakesha as she stared at Peter.

"Thank you," said Peter, as he rubbed Nakesha's finger.

"Hey Peter, I want to talk to you about something," she said to him.

"Can it wait? I'm about to start my ritual," said Hush.

"I guess," she said.

"What is it about?" he asked.

"Just that, I think we need to stop while we can; you have a lot of money, so I don't see why not," said Nakesha.

Peter looked at her and said, "Kesha, babes, are you freezing up on me?"

"No, but those FBI guys do scare me sometimes," she said.

"It's FTC, not FBI. But listen, Kesha; everything will be okay. What could go wrong?" he asked.

"Don't you know I'm protected by the dead?" he further asked.

"Peter, you know I don't believe in that voodoo shit," she replied.

"Oh yeah, even though your parents are originally from New Orleans?" he asked.

"Actually, my dad is Haitian, and my mom is from New Orleans," she said.

"Even better, Voodoo is well known in Haiti," he said. "Just trust in the dead; they will protect us from the FBI like you said," said Peter as he laughed at Nakesha.

"Peter, I'm serious. At least take a break after this one," she said.

"Okay, Kesha, go wait for me outside and practice your manager's voice," he said to her.

She left; he was now wrapping his head with the white cloth, wrapping it like a turban. He then put two pencils between his ears, he then took a shot of white rum, gargled, then swallowed, then suddenly, his eyes started to roll back into his head. You could see the white parts of his eyes as he chanted a very strange prayer. Nakesha kept walking.

Nakesha, now making her way downstairs, realized Tamika and Calvin were missing. She called out for Tamika, but she heard nothing. She walked closer to the back. She heard moaning and grunting coming from the back steps. She got outside and saw Calvin fucking Tamika with her legs up in the air. Calvin's pants were down; he had taken his red, green, and gold mesh marina off and put his rachet knife on the car.

"Shit," said Nakesha as she saw Calvin ramming Tamika. She quickly ran back in.

"Hey, Calvin, was that Nakesha?" she asked, but Calvin was still fucking her; Calvin stabbed; she moaned.

"Yeah, man, a she man, don't move baby, mi soon cum in a yuh," said Calvin.

"Calvin, please stop, man," said Tamika as she pushed him off.

"A what happens to you my girl," said Calvin "Yuh pussy feel good pon mi cocky," he further said. Tamika then blushed. He then tried to slip it back in.

"Could you stop acting like a prick? We can always fuck another time. You lucky yah dick is big, Calvin," she said.

"Save mi number as 'big dick Calvin,'" he said to her as he pulled his pants up.

11 AM

Moments later, they both got dressed and went back into the living room. Tamika went and sat down. Calvin then walked toward the circle of candles, where he stood behind them in between the caged chickens. Calvin looked at Tamika while he grabbed his crotch; she looked away.

"You were moaning really hard," said Nakesha.

Tamika smiled, "OMG!" she said.

Then there were footsteps; Peter was now making his way down the stairs, looking like a ghost, in a long white gown, white turban, and with a bible. He walked past the girls and got into the circle. He was now sitting down in the circle of candles. He then nodded to Calvin; Calvin nodded back, and then the strangest thing happened.

Calvin quickly opened the cage and aggressively pulled both chickens out. Holding them tightly by the neck, he took his 3-star rachet out, cut both their necks, and their heads fell off. The girls got disgusted and looked away.

"Isn't this a bit harsh, wouldn't you say?" Tamika asked Nakesha, "Is this really necessary?" she further said while she continued to turn away from all the blood spraying from the chicken's neck. "Bloody 'ell man, we only calling on some rich old geezer, Jesus Christ, mate," she further said.

"I told Peter I don't believe in this voodoo shit," said Nakesha. "I really hate this part," she further said.

"NUH MORE BOMBOCLAAT TALKING," Calvin shouted as he looked at the women.

"That guy scares me sometimes," said Nakesha.

He then sprinkled the blood of the chicken in a circle around Peter, poured some into a cup, and gave it to him. Hush drank it in one go, then wiped some on his face. Calvin then stepped back and put the dead chicken in a bag.

"Curry chicken lata," he said to himself, blood all over his red, green, and gold mesh marina, his jeans, and his desert Clarks. He put the bag down, then turned around and said, "CHOP E LINE NOW."

Hush nodded, then started to chant something in Nigerian—over and over, he chanted, over and over. His eyes went back in his head. He then kissed a ring on his finger, a ring he called the "Guard Ring." According to Peter, dead spirits were stored in this ring, which protected him from any physical and supernatural harm.

He then stopped. The place became completely silent.

"The dead is here to assist," he said. He then dialed a number from a piece of paper. The phone started to ring. Ring, ring, ring, ring. It was ringing.

Nakesha realized Peter didn't have the lead sheet. "Pete, your sheet," she whispered while the phone rang.

"I don't need it," he said, and then someone answered. Peter quickly reverted his attention from Nakesha to the call.

"Hello, Rhonda, speaking," said the caller.

"Hello, good morning, is this Ms. Rhonda Speight speaking?" Peter asked the "skull,"—that is the name he gave the people that he scammed.

"Yes, Rhonda here. Who is this?" Rhonda asked.

"Hello, Mrs. Speight. How do you do today?" Peter asked.

"Not good, my cat just died," Rhonda replied.

"What is the name of your cat?" Peter asked.

"Her name is Lady Diva. Who is this?" Rhonda asked again, with a concerned tone.

Calvin quickly looked at Hush. Peter now realized he was losing the "skull," Calvin then sprayed an oily fragrance around Peter and said a strange word. "Shalama," said Calvin, then Peter spoke.

"Well, Mrs. Speight, what if I told you I could make your day brighter than the sun?" said Peter.

"What do you mean?" Rhonda asked.

"Well, Mrs. Speight, your name has popped up in our lucky Walmart customer list, and you have won a million dollars. What would you say to that?" Peter asked Rhonda.

"OMG!" said Rhonda while she screamed in joy. "Are you serious?" she further asked.

By now, Tamika and Nakesha were both smiling, as Peter whispered to them—"Shhh," he said with his index finger over his mouth.

"But Mrs. Speight, you will need to pay $100,000.00 for a holder's fee," said Peter. Peter then wrote Rhonda's full name in cursive writing on the bottom of his feet and then stepped on the ground.

"Ashalama Kallama," he said in a whisper.

"No problem. What is 100,000 to a million? Where do I send it?" Rhonda asked Peter.

"My manager will handle that part. Her name is Sarah Conway," said Peter. "Have a great day, Mrs. Speight, and I hope you spend that money wisely," Peter further said to her. He handed the phone to Tamika.

"Hello, Mrs. Speight. Sarah Conway here, manager for Lennord County Walmart. Congratulations on your winnings. What will you do with all this money?" Tamika asked in her New York accent.

"Geeze, my hands are shaking just thinking about it," said Rhonda. "I know a million isn't what it used to be, so with that said, I would just hire a good financial person," she further said. Tamika made the insane mind gesture.

"That is right, Mrs. Speight," said Tamika as Sarah Conway.

"I'm ready whenever you are ready, Mrs. Speight," Tamika further said as she sat in front of her laptop. By now, Peter was still sitting and chanting strange words.

Rhonda then told Tamika all her bank information, one by one. She listed the details of her personal banking information. Everything went well, and the money had been lodged in Lennord County Savings Bank, the bank Nakesha worked at.

"Okay, Mrs. Speight, you will receive a million dollars in your bank account in 24 hours," said Tamika.

"Oh, thank you, my dear," said Rhonda.

She then hung up. "Stupid cunt," said Tamika, while she took the sim card out of the phone, broke it in two, and tossed the phone into the fire. Then Peter shouted.

"SHE JUST GOT CHOPPED!"

After every successful scam, the four must make a withdrawal from four different bank accounts. Nakeisha, who was already dressed for work, went in and acted as the teller for the four bank account users—it was 25 thousand each. And that style of scamming is called "chopping the line."

Let's go to scam number 2. This one is called the "tear the bank" scam—what a name.

TEAR THE BANK

This is where Peter had Nakesha secretly withdrawing $1.50 from Lennord County locals, and if upon withdrawing and none of the customers caught on, they took up to $100 every two months. But this one didn't last too long—Nakesha was too scared to continue due to a certain incident. Now let us revisit that incident.

JUNE 2004

It was a regular day for Nakesha at work. There she sat, just doing her teller job, then suddenly an irate customer burst in, cussing up a storm, arguing about some money that had been taken out of her account, and she demanded to speak to the bank manager. Nakesha overheard the customer and started to panic,

"Ma'am, what is the problem?" Nakesha asked the customer.

"I need my fucking money; someone took money out of my account," said the customer.

Nakesha was nervous as hell because she knew exactly what the "skull" was talking about, but she wasn't all that worried. That is because of what Peter had told her to do if this situation ever happened. What is that, you might ask?

Peter had instructed Nakesha to text him immediately when this happened with the customer's name.

Why the name?

You see, Peter had something set up where if a customer's money was missing, and that customer was on his list, he could make it look like someone was using the customer's card from way out of town. In other words, if the FTC fraud squad was looking at the missing money, it would appear as if someone from the west coast was using the customer's card to purchase an unknown app.

The manager came out.

"Ma'am, I'm the manager. My name is Casey McCarthy. How may I help you?" she asked. "What is your name?" she further asked.

"Silvia Conn," said the irate customer.

Nakesha heard the name and quickly texted Peter.

"Peter, Silvia Conn just came in complaining about her money," she texted. The customer then went into Casey's office.

Peter wrote then Nakesha back. "Kesha, this name is not in my system," Peter texted.

"What the hell you mean?" Nakesha texted back while she panicked.

"Nakesha, I said you didn't give me this name," Peter texted her.

"Then why is she arguing about money, then Peter?" she said.

"If I get caught, I don't know what I would do. Peter, so you better be right," said Nakesha.

Moments later, the customer was now coming back out. She shook the manager's hands, said thank you to her, and then left.

"Nakesha, can I see you in my office?" said Casey.

She then went to the manager's office. She was in there in there for like a good 10 minutes. Moments after she came back out, the other tellers looked at her like, "What the fuck is going on?" Nakesha walked back toward her desk. "I got to stop tearing the bank and stick to chopping the line," she whispered to herself. She got back to her seat.

"Nakesha, what happened?" one teller asked her.

"That bitch had an overdraft fee of $25 dollars for not having enough money in her bank account," said Nakesha, both the tellers started laughing.

"I thought it was another scam," said the teller. "Scamming has become a problem in Lennord County. Just last week, I heard some people talking about a man named, the Top Scammer," she further said. "Have you heard about that, Nicky?" she further asked.

"Nope, never have," Nakesha replied.

NOW BACK TO 2005, JUNE, TO BE SPECIFIC.

Everything was going well for Peter and his friends, making millions of dollars and flooding the whole of Lennord County with money. With all the attention, Peter tried to stay in mostly, but he did come out now and then, when he needed to go to the grocery store.

2 MONTHS LATER
ANOTHER (LCNS) PRESS RELEASE

The News Anchor speaks: "It doesn't look like this scamming pandemic is getting any better. What is FTC doing? Is the government part of this scamming pandemic? Is that the reason why they stay dormant?" the news anchor asked.

It looks like the government was watching the Lennord County news, because just two weeks after that press release, the government had released another press release about an invention that would save the county from scamming. They had now come up with a new app that could show a number as likely a scam whenever there is an incoming. This app was called the "ROBOCALL."

Watching all of this were Peter, Calvin, Tamika, and Nakesha from a cabin in Glasco, Sage Town.

"Well, mates, it has been a good run," said Tamika.

"EVERYTHING WILL BE FINE," said Peter, with full confidence.

"Peter, nothing lasts forever. Maybe this is a sign for us to stop," said Nakesha.

"Could you not start with that again? If you want to go, just go—we all know you are a traitor," said Peter.

"And what the fuck do you mean by that?" Nakesha asked while she looked at Peter strongly.

"Remember back in 2004? Remember what you said?" Peter asked Nakesha.

Everyone was now looking at Nakesha. "A weh she seh Peter?" Calvin asked.

"She said if she gets caught, she doesn't know what she would do," said Peter.

"A weh di bomboclaat yah seh to mi, Peter," said Calvin as he started to get angry.

"You don't remember when you said that?" Peter asked Nakesha.

"I was scared," said Nakesha.

"And that is exactly why you are a potential informer," Peter replied. Nakesha then got mad and started to walk out. Tamika got up also.

"Bye," said Peter and Calvin. She paid them no mind.

"You guys can be wankers sometime, you know that?" said Tamika. Then Nakesha turned back around.

"You know what? Fuck you, Peter," said Nakesha. "I have paid my debt to you. I owe you nothing. I'm done," said Nakesha. While she quickly walked out, Tamika hesitated not.

"Calvin, your dick is big, but your attitude stinks," said Tamika and walked off.

One week later…

Neither Peter nor Calvin heard anything from Tamika or Nakesha.

Unfortunately, it seemed like the girls weren't the only thing that had left the Top Scammer and his friend.

Week after week, Peter was failing like crazy, not because he was not good at it anymore, but because no one was answering anymore. The "Robocall," app was working great. According to the government, it's the best thing since sliced bread. Seems like Hush's voodoo wasn't strong enough.

Peter now fully convinced himself that he must take a different approach. He had decided to put "CHOP THE LINE," scamming on hold and do more "TEAR THE BANK," until he figured something out. Oh wait, he can't tear the bank either. Nakesha was M.I.A. She was nowhere to be found; she even left her job. She had skipped town with Tamika, and Tamika had taken Nakesha back to Aston Villa, Birmingham, just off Aston Brook Street, close to the football field.

2 MONTHS LATER

Peter and Calvin were hanging at the mansion, watching English Premier League, Chelsea vs. Liverpool; Calvin had run out of rolling paper.

"Kick the bomboclaat ball enuh Drogba," said Calvin. "it's Steven Gerrard for me all day," said Hush.

"Yo, Peter," said Calvin.

"Yo, German," said Peter.

"Mi a guh get a Bob Marley rolling paper, by Stewart, yah come wid me?" Calvin asked Peter.

"Yes, why not?" he replied.

Moments later, they both jumped in a black X6. Calvin was driving. They drove off. Calvin then lit his last spliff. He took a puff and passed it to Peter. Hush took it and took several puffs from it but was still holding on to the spliff.

"Peter, pass di bomboclaat weed nuh man," said Calvin. Peter then passed him back the spliff and turned the music up.

It was Tenor Saw's "Ring the Alarm," played; they smoked and sang all the way to Lenni Deli instead.

Moments later, they were both in Lenni Deli; Dancehall music was coming through the Deli speaker—"Gimme the Light," by Sean Paul.

"Yah yard, man?" Calvin asked the shopkeeper.

"Yes, I am," he replied.

"Big up yuhself then," said Calvin.

"Let me get one a dem Bob rolling paper," he further asked.

"Sorry, my man, I'm out of Bob; this one guy keeps buying them out," he said.

"Who?" Calvin asked.

"I think his name is Andre Paul; he is a local writer," he replied. "When I tell you, man, he buys papers a lot, he must smoke a lot," said the shopkeeper.

"Well, if him a writer, him must smoke whole lot a weed, mi wudda love fi meet him," said Calvin.

"Well, you are in luck; he is right across the street—that is Andre Paul," said the shopkeep as he pointed at a man through the window, standing over by Barnes & Noble.

Moments later, Calvin and Peter were finished with the store and were now leaving, Calvin making his way to Andre Paul.

Suddenly, a black minivan pulled up in front of them. Peter and Calvin were frightened. Calvin pulled out his 3-star Rachet knife.

"Pussy weh una do," said Calvin.

Andre Paul was now looking at what was going on, dressed in purple flannel with black tuxedo pants and a purple bandana tied around his head, making his way to the scene when he heard.

"Suck unu mother," said Calvin.

Then one of the men then took out a tranquilizer gun and shot both Peter and Calvin, and quickly tossed them in a black van. They took them to a big garage in the middle of an open field, strung them up, and stripped them naked, leaving them in just underwear while their feet swung in the air. Peter and Calvin were now waking up only to find themselves tied up. When he looked up, he saw a group of people.

"A weh di bomboclaat una wah wid wi?" Calvin asked. "Shut up, you scamming piece of shit," said a male voice.

They both looked up and while they swung naked, they saw what could be over 50 old people standing and waiting with whips in their hands. Then a voice spoke.

"Mr. Peter Hush, a.k.a Top Scammer, the man who says, 'chop the line,'" said the voice.

"Calvin Blake, the original rude boy from Kingston," he further said. "You think we wouldn't catch up to you! You think you could scam all these honest working people of Lennord County and get away with it," he said. "After we are done here, no one will ever hear from you two again." He further stated.

He then played a tape, replaying all the voices Peter used to scam everyone.

Peter listened while he and Calvin swung naked, left to right. Peter then looked up; he saw a government badge that said "FBI."

"Ladies and gentlemen, it's your show," said the FBI official.

Then suddenly, the entire flock of old people walked down to Peter and Calvin and started to lash them relentlessly—nonstop, they lashed while he cried out in pain.

"Bomboclaat," said Calvin as they whipped him.

"Where is your black magic now?" said the FBI agent.

Blood was now dripping from their bodies, lash marks all over, and they started to lash them again and again. They all stopped; the officer then instructed the old people to put their whips down and leave the room.

Moments after, the room was cleared. The FBI agent then walked up to Peter and Calvin, pulling his gun out. He placed a tape recorder on the ground, then pressed play. It started to play, and the FBI agent then shot both Peter and Calvin in the head. He walked away, leaving the tape still running on the end of the tape; you could hear:

"YOU GUYS DON'T NEED TO WORRY, AND WE WILL PUT YOU IN WITNESS PROTECTION SOMEWHERE IN ENGLAND. JUST TELL US HOW TO CATCH PETER HUSH AND CALVIN BLAKE. PLEASE SIGN HERE. INFORMANT: NAKESHA BARNS AND TAMIKA COSWELL,"

Made in the USA
Columbia, SC
27 June 2024

f1954d63-2e0d-4e93-9556-27b4db878c41R01